COKE GURLS 2: CHI-TOWN

AJ DIX

D1519337

TEXT UCP TO 22828 TO SUBSCRIBE TO OUR MAILING LIST
If you would like to join our team, submit the first 3-4 chapters of your completed manuscript to
Submissions@UrbanChapterspublications.com

ACKNOWLEDGMENTS

Dee Ann & Brii: You two are always my shoulder to lean on and I appreciate that, especially in a world full of shady people. When I'm feeling discouraged, you two always get me together and help me realize my dopeness. I'm happy to call you my friends!

To the best publisher in the world, Jahquel: I can't thank you enough for believing in me enough to give me a chance. Although you always tell my mama on me, I forgive you. Lol. You can't get rid of me and I'm here for liiiiffeee!

To my readers: Thank you for constantly sticking with me through this journey as I continue to grow. It took me a while to finish this finale because I wanted to make sure it was perfect for y'all and every question was answered. Yes, this really is the end for these crazy women, and I hope you enjoy it!

Don't forget to leave reviews!

From Part One...

Echo "EJ"

"Yeah?" I mumbled into the phone. I was in the middle of some good-ass sleep when my phone kept ringing, back to back.

"Yo, EJ, I need you to come down to Grandma's house," Looney said, speaking in code.

I opened my eyes and saw it was a little after midnight. "G, for what? This ain't nothing you can handle?" I asked, annoyed.

"Nah, she sick."

"A'ight, man, here I come." I hung up and got out the bed, dragging my feet across the floor. My stomach was poking out more as I was now in my second trimester of pregnancy. My stomach poked out a little, but I was still able to hide it under a large t-shirt.

After throwing on some sweats and a pair of Air Max, I left the house. It didn't take me long to get to the warehouse we had on 87th and Kedzie. When I saw only Looney and Moe's cars parked outside, I knew it was about to be some bullshit.

"Man, I swear on my life I didn't do it." I heard an unknown voice say on the verge of tears.

"Shut uuuppp, nigga." That voice belonged to Moe.

"What the fuck y'all want?" I snapped as I stood in front of these two fools and one of my runners.

"We got a call from Nate in Indianapolis and he said shipment was short," Moe explained. "Now, I might be a little off sometimes, but a bitch knows how to count very well."

"You double checked it?" I asked, looking at Looney.

"Yeah."

"So, can one of y'all tell me why the fuck he still breathing, and I'm out of my bed at this time of night?"

"Look, you said we need to be mindful of the bodies that's dropping, so I wanted to run it by you."

Pow!

I shot the guy in the middle of his forehead and turned to leave. "Problem solved. Now, don't wake me up no more," I called out over my shoulder.

"Them babies got her mean as fuck," Moe mumbled.

"I heard that, heffa!"

"Good!"

Looney and Moe were having a good ol' time laughing as I left the warehouse. I didn't feel like going home, so I drove to Malik's house.

We were still in a weird space, but he kept up his end and came to every doctor's appointment.

I pulled into Malik's driveway and parked behind his car. I had gotten a key made for when I wanted to randomly come over at night, so I let myself in.

"The fuck?"

I jumped when I heard Malik's voice, and saw him sitting on the couch, watching TV.

"What you doing up?" I took my shoes off and left them at the door.

"How about, how did you get in my house?" There was some amusement in his tone as he looked at me.

"With a key. Duh. I'm going to bed."

I stripped out of my clothes and got under the covers. Malik's ass liked to sleep with the fan on, and the last time I did that, I woke up sick.

"I'ma need that key back, Echo. You can't just popup whenever you feel like it," Malik complained.

"Okay, next time, I'll go to my other nigga's house when I don't feel like going home." I didn't hear anything, so I figured Malik had left the room. "Aaah!" I shrieked when Malik snatched me up out the bed.

"Why do you gotta play so much? You like getting me out of character, don't you?" He huffed in my face.

"Yeah, daddy, I love that shit." I blew an air kiss at him and he let me go. "The next time you grab me like that, I'm going to shoot you in your ass."

"You know it's against the law to threaten me, right?" Malik got on his side of the bed and slid under the covers.

"Now you know I never gave a fuck about no laws. Goodnight, baby daddy." I yawned and got back comfortable. Hopefully, I could go back to having a peaceful sleep with no distractions.

€

The next morning, I got up and I was in bed alone. It was quiet in the house, making me believe Malik was gone. Before I went to do my investigation, I had to empty my bladder before I had an accident.

After handling my hygiene, I walked to the front of the house to see if Malik was there. I didn't see him, and when I looked outside, my truck was gone, too. "No, the fuck he didn't," I said aloud. I stalked back to the room to get my phone. Malik had lost his rabid ass mind if he thought he was just going to take my ride and go whenever he pleased.

"About time you got up," Malik complained into the phone.

"Where are you with my truck, Malik?"

"Maaan, don't start when you got a whole key made to my crib. I'm on my way back," Malik said, then hung up the phone.

"Rude bastard," I scoffed.

I sat, waiting at the door for Malik to come back, so I could leave. I thought about giving him a piece of my mind for hanging up on me, but I decided not to even bother.

"Here." When Malik walked through the door, he tossed a bag at me.

"What's this for?" I asked, peeking in the bag.

"We're about to meet my folks for lunch. Get changed," he demanded.

"I'm good on that. I'd rather go home."

"Look, this is important for my mama, so you're coming, even if I got to handcuff you. So, you can go voluntarily or involuntarily. Your choice," he stated.

I stared on in shock. What's up with everybody trying to kidnap me and shit?

After I got dressed, we left the house and ended up at Gibson's Steakhouse. I was silent the whole ride because I really didn't want to be here. When I made eye contact with Police Superintendent Stevens, the little voice in my head told me to leave.

"Heeyyy, Echo. I've been trying to reach you for the longest." Malani greeted me first with a hug.

"It's been crazy. I'm sorry about that," I half-lied.

"Being a criminal is time consuming," his father mumbled.

I had to remember who he was and where we were because I was about to go across his head. If it was one thing he knew about me, he knew how I felt about my respect.

"Martin, stop it," Victoria warned. "How are you, sweetie?" She gave me a half-smile as I took my seat.

"I'm good, and yourself?"

"I was lucky enough to open my eyes this morning, so I'm blessed."

"Since everybody is going to be rude, I guess I'll introduce myself. I'm Martin Jr., and this is my wife, Tamia."

I just gave them a half-smile and continued to look over the menu. I seemed to be invisible at this table because they were busy laughing and joking with each other while I sat, sipping my water. This shit was awkward as hell, and I was three seconds from snatching Tamia's eyeballs out since she didn't know where they belonged.

"Do you have something on your mind?" I directed my question to Tamia, who looked shocked.

"Excuse me?"

"You're excused. Now, why are you staring at me?"

Malik rubbed my thigh to calm me down, but that did nothing.

"You just look familiar, that's all. I didn't mean to offend anyone." She didn't think I missed her rolling those bubble-ass eyes at me, but I'd handle that later.

"Why am I here?" I whispered to Malik.

"I haven't told them about the babies yet," Malik admitted.

I looked to him with squinted eyes. The hell did he mean, he didn't tell them? "Okay, well, let me stop wasting my time here," I announced, standing up. "Me and Malik are having a baby; well, babies. Enjoy your food." Grabbing my purse, I walked off from the table and walked quickly away from the restaurant, so I could order an Uber or something.

"Echo, hold up," Malik called out as he jogged to me. "Where are you going?"

"Home. If I stay here, I'm going to end up putting a slug in yo' dad and sister-in-law. We don't have to do this family shit. You made it clear we were going to co-parent, so don't try to force a relationship with your family on me. Clearly, the line has been getting crossed the last few weeks, and that's my fault. From now on, if it doesn't have anything to do with the babies, we have nothing to talk about. Enjoy the rest of your day." With that being said, I hopped in my ride that had just pulled up.

NAOMI "NA"

"Well, Naomi, I hope you're ready, because it's looking like your little one will be making his arrival today or tomorrow," Dr. Evelyn said as she finished my ultrasound.

"Why? I still got three weeks until my due date."

"The fluid around the baby is low, and that could cause some major problems down the line, like infections. Don't worry, though, you just go on over to the main hospital to get checked in and we'll start this induction."

Dr. Evelyn left the room and I looked to Jamal with tears in my eyes.

"What you about to cry for, Na?"

"I don't want anything to be wrong with my baby," I cried.

"Sssshhh. It ain't nothing wrong with my li'l soldier. He just ready to get up out of there." Jamal assured as he kissed me on my forehead.

"I guess you right. Come on so we can call the girls."

Jamal helped me down carefully and we made our way over to the hospital. I called Echo and my sisters, and they arrived just as I got hooked up with the Pitocin. That shit was no joke, because it seemed like five minutes after they started the IV, I was having contractions.

"Ohhh," I moaned out in pain as a contraction ripped through my body.

"You gotta breathe through it, baby. Remember how they showed us in the class?" Jamal was standing in my face, huffing and puffing like the big bad wolf, and I wanted to stab him in the neck.

"Man, that shit ain't gon' work," Looney said, laughing.

"Looney, sit yo' ass down. You act like you had kids before," Echo finally spoke. She had been sitting next to my bed, but had been quiet since she'd gotten here.

"Everything okay?" I asked Echo once my contraction was gone.

"How are you sitting here worried about me when you're the one in labor? I'm good, just patiently waiting on my godson." I could tell Echo was hiding something, and I would get to the bottom of it another time.

I was in labor for eleven hours before I was told it was time to push. By this time, it was only me, Jamal, and Echo in the room. Echo's weird ass was standing at the end of the bed, while Jamal refused to go past my shoulders.

"Okay, Naomi, I'm going to count down from ten and I want you to give me a big push," Dr. Evelyn instructed.

I was pushing for an hour and this little boy was acting like he wasn't trying to come out. "I can't do this. I can't do this," I panted.

"Come on, Naomi, if you don't push him out, you'll have to get a cesarean, and I know that's not what you want. Grab behind your knees and give me a big push like you're on the toilet."

"Ten... nine... eight... seven... six..."

"Aahh!" I screamed and pushed as hard as I could until they got to one.

"Good job! Keep going," Dr. Evelyn encouraged.

"Oh my—eck! Un-un, eck! I got to get out of here." Echo was gagging as she ran out the door.

"That's why I stayed my ass up here," Jamal pointed out.

After two more big pushes, my son, Jamal Jr., was finally brought into this world. He was screaming at the top of his lungs, but that was like music to my ears. I knew right then and there I would break my back to make sure he was happy at all times.

"Thank you so much, Na." Jamal kissed me all over my face and I could've sworn I felt some of his tears on my face.

I would clown him later, but right now, it was all about our young prince.

∞

"How long has he been crying like that?" Jamal asked as he walked into the room.

"For the past thirty minutes, and I don't know what to do for him," I whined. We'd been home for three days and I felt like I was failing as a parent already. Jamal Jr. had been screaming like somebody was pinching him and nothing was soothing him.

"Call his doctor or something," Jamal suggested as he tapped away on his phone.

"That's the reason I called you, so you can take us." I rolled my eyes as I handed JJ to Jamal.

"Come on, don't start that nagging."

"Nigga, the last thing I do is nag. I just think you need to be a little more present with this baby. Since we been home, you've been spending all this time out, then come in late. I'm tired of being the only one getting up for these feedings."

"I'm out here securing a bag for us. Why you tripping, Na?"

"Just put him in his car seat so I can finish getting dressed." I waved him off as I slipped on my sweats. After making sure I had everything in the diaper bag, we left out.

The entire ride to the doctor's office, Jamal's phone buzzed nonstop. Whoever it was, Jamal was screening the hell out of their calls.

"You not gon' get that?" I asked, pointing to the phone in the cupholder.

"Nah, it's just them niggas at the studio, and I know they don't want shit. I'm going back once we done here anyway."

"Mmmhhmm." See what I mean? He couldn't even sit the hell still for a second.

When we made it to the doctor's office, I checked JJ in and took a seat. I kept feeling like someone was watching me, so I quickly did a scan of the room. I made eye contact with a woman who was eyeing me like I'd killed her favorite puppy. She looked familiar, but I just couldn't place where I had seen her.

"My boobs are leaking, I got to go pump," I said to Jamal as I grabbed the diaper bag and went to the bathroom. JJ had finally calmed down and was sleeping, so I was not about to wake him up.

Once I emptied my boobs enough so it wasn't uncomfortable, I went back to the waiting room. Imagine my surprise when I saw the same broad arguing with Jamal.

"Um, can I help you?" I interrupted their quarrel.

"No, you can't," this bitch had the nerve to say.

"I think you misunderstood what I was saying. Bitch, you need to move around before you wake my baby up."

"You're just going to let her talk to me like that?" she asked, shocked.

"Who is this?" I directed my question to Jamal, who seemed to be sweating all of a sudden. I got another look at this bitch who obviously couldn't take a hint and tried to place where I knew her from.

"Na, come on." Jamal stood up and tried to reach for my hand, but I stepped back.

"Okay, since you can't talk, I'll let her know. I'm the mother of your son's little sister." She rubbed her stomach and it was then that I noticed her baby bump.

"Come again?" I cocked my head to the side and stared at Jamal. I felt my eye twitching, and I just knew I was about to catch a body.

"I said I'm—oh my God!"

Click.

"Na, put the gun down. You can't do that in here," Jamal urged as I pointed my gun in this bitch's face.

"This the same bitch you said you never touched." I laughed evilly as the realization set in of where I knew her from. "Give me your keys," I demanded.

Jamal slowly handed me his car keys and I snatched my baby's car seat up to leave. Jamal was begging and pleading for me to stop and talk to him, but I wouldn't. If he valued his life, he'd better leave me alone.

"Freeze! Put the weapon down!" I heard as I stepped outside. There was a squad car parked outside and the officers had their weapons drawn on me.

"Fuck," I cursed as I laid the gun on the ground. Jamal was going to feel me after this.

1

NAOMI "NA"

"Breaking someone's trust is like crumpling up a perfect piece of paper. You can smooth it over but it's never going to be the same again." -Unknown

"LISTEN, I could get in trouble for this, but I know who you are. I'm going to give you your gun back, but I'm taking the ammunition." The officer who was standing by the car with me was rambling, and I just nodded to get him to hurry up.

"Thank you," I mumbled, then walked off. Jamal was standing by his car with JJ. I still had his key, so I knew he wasn't going anywhere.

"Are you gon' talk, or you about to show yo' ass?" Jamal asked. He was eyeing me like he had a problem, and I was ready to go upside his head.

"You better put my baby in this car and get away from me," I warned. I hoped he didn't think he was free from anything.

"How the fuck I'm supposed to move around if you in my whip?"

"I don't give a fuck, honestly." I pushed passed him and got in the driver's seat. He was smart and did what I said. I pulled away and headed toward Ki's clinic. I was mad I had let them distract me from the reason I was out in the first place.

"Hey, Naomi. Oh, my goodness, you had the baby," Kiarra cooed as she came around the desk.

"Yes, he's three days old and he's crying like somebody's killing him." I ran down the reason we were here, and she led us back to a room.

"Strip him down for me," Kiarra instructed as she washed her hands. I held JJ in my lap as she looked him over. "Okay, he just seems to be gassy," Kiarra announced.

"Gas? That's it?"

"Yeah, you can get some gripe water and he'll be okay, trust me. I will tell you to watch what you eat, though."

I let out a huge sigh of relief. "Thank you so much. I never knew having a newborn would be so hard."

"It's a learning thing. You're doing fine, just relax," Kiarra reassured me with a smile

After getting JJ redressed, we left and headed to EJ's loft. That was where she'd been spending majority of her time, and I knew it was because of the guy who waits on her hand and foot. Echo still hadn't been back to *The Gallery*, and I think she was going to sell it. Right now, her focus had been on carrying the babies, and I couldn't blame her.

"Hey, Scott." I waved at Echo's favorite concierge and walked to the elevator.

The door opened as I stood in front of it, and Echo smiled at us. "Hey, my favorite people," Echo cooed.

"Hey, bestie. I got to tell you about this bullshit with Jamal," I ranted as I got comfortable on the couch.

"What he do?"

"So, you know the entire reason we broke up was because of the girl in the trap house. This nigga lied and said he never touched this girl, and we run into her today and the bitch say she pregnant by him."

"Where the hell was this?!" EJ shrieked, getting hyped in her seat.

"At the doctor's office," I sighed. "I wasn't thinking, and I pulled my gun out. Thankfully, the officer outside knew us and let me go."

"Girl, I don't blame you because I probably would've reacted the same way. I can't tell you the stuff I almost got into because of my feelings. They would've shared a bullet."

"He better be lucky my son needs a father, or I would kill him." I meant every word I said. I told Jamal if he messed up, I was killing him. But I'd rather make his ass suffer for life. JJ was acting like he was hungry, so I unsnapped my shirt to feed him.

"I can't believe I'll have two babies to feed and take care of. This has got to be a sick joke." Echo laughed, and I joined in.

"I know, right, but I know you'll be a wonderful mother. How's the Malik situation?" I asked. From the way she rolled her eyes, I knew it wasn't good.

"I haven't heard from him since he forced me to that lunch with his family. He's been calling me, but I told his ass we don't have nothing to talk about unless it's about these two," Echo said, rubbing her swollen belly.

"Well, you know you got help when you need it. How's pregnancy treating you right now?"

"I'm over the sickness finally. I love feeling them both move around." Echo's face lit up as she spoke. No matter how rough she had it growing up, I know my best friend was going to be a great mother.

I stayed with Echo until me and JJ started to get sleepy. After picking up the gripe water from Walgreens, I ordered a salad to be delivered when I got home. I was happy that Jamal didn't have his ass at my house when I got there because I would've had to show my ass, again.

2

ECHO "EJ"

"Women in this business cannot afford to look weak." -Camila Vargas

KNOCK. *Knock.*

"Come on, man," I groaned as I got up from the couch. I hated to get up after I had already found my comfortable spot. "Can I help you?" I sassed as I opened the door. Malik stood there, looking like he was about get on my nerves.

"You don't know how to answer yo' phone no more?" Malik barked as he walked inside.

"Don't question me. I didn't answer my phone because I didn't want to. I meant what I told you the other day."

"Look, I want to apologize for that. I don't want us to go to a place we can't get back from. I want to work on this." Malik motioned between us. "We need to try for them."

"What is there to work on? Can you honestly say you can accept me, knowing what I do for a living, and what you do for a living?" I asked him.

"Yeah, as far as I'm concerned, you're Echo the artist, and I'm just Detective Stevens. We're going to go back to keeping our professional lives out of our relationship. Is that cool with you?"

Everything inside told me to say yeah and run off into the sunset with him, but I couldn't let myself be vulnerable like that again. Being in love caused me to slip and it could've cost me everything. I'd never let myself get there again.

"I can't do it," I said lowly with my head down. I wanted to avoid the sad look I knew was on his face.

"Why not? I know you're not still mad about that shit with my dad?"

I finally looked him in his eyes and I wished I hadn't. "I just don't think we can work out. I mean, we're kind of tied for life with the twins, but to be in a relationship again just won't work. Too much has been said and done."

"I'm standing here saying I can forget and forgive everything; you can't?" Malik's voice raised an octave, and he looked at me like I had extra heads. His handsome face was screwed up in a sexy-ass mug. These babies had my hormones all over the place. I was ready to take him down in here.

"I said how I felt about the situation and I don't plan on changing my mind. Can you lock the door on your way out, please?" My doctor had told me about remaining stress free, so I wasn't about to go back and forth with him. I went to my kitchen and waited until I heard the door slam.

Malik might be in his feelings for a minute, but it was what was best for the both of us until I left the game completely.

$$\maltese$$

A FEW NIGHTS LATER...

AFTER TOSSING and turning half the night, I finally drifted off to a good sleep, only to be woken up with my business and personal phones going off.

"What?!" I screamed into the first phone I picked up.

"EJ, shit is bad, man. Niggas is trying us, you need to get down here," Moe huffed into the phone.

"Is. Somebody. Fucking. Dead?" I spoke slowly and clearly.

"No, but Looney got hit. I-I think I stopped the bleeding, but I got to get her out of here."

"What the fuck?! Why you didn't lead with that? I don't know where you at, but you gon' have to pick her little ass up and bring her to the address I send you. Moe, keep yo' shit together and get there safely." I hung up and got out the bed as quickly as I could.

"Ow, shit," I groaned as I felt a sharp pain shoot through my back. After a few seconds, the pain went away, so I continued to throw some clothes on to leave. I couldn't even leave shit alone to enjoy pregnancy without having to come out of retirement every three fucking seconds. I sent Moe the address to the doctor I kept on payroll for times like this, then met them there.

"EJ, I don't know what the fuck happened. We was leaving from doing a pickup and niggas tried to rush in the house. Shit happened quick." Moe was rambling and pacing the floor as we waited for the doctor to get done with Looney. Thankfully, the bullet in her shoulder went in and out and she was going to live.

"Chill, Moe. Them niggas just better look worse than she do," I said calmly.

"I know for a fact we took two of 'em down before the other ones bolted."

"Where the fuck is my money?"

"In the house still. I didn't have time to lock it up."

"What the fuck? I know you not that fuckin' slow? Them niggas could've doubled back when you left. I swear—" My sentence was cut short when another sharp pain shot through my body, making me bend over in pain.

"EJ, you good?" Moe tried to reach out for my arm, but I shook her off.

"Go grab who you can and empty the fuckin' house out. Take it to the warehouse and I'll deal with the rest tomorrow," I said in between deep breaths.

"I can handle it if you want. You got it, boss lady." Moe took heed to the death glare I shot at her and threw her hands up in mock surrender before backing out the room.

I sighed and took my seat. I rubbed circles on my belly to calm my nerves. This shit wasn't random, and when I found out who had decided to fuck with me and mine, it was about to be a lot of slow singing and flower bringing around this bitch.

"All right, Echo, she's all patched up and high as a kite," Dr. Krane announced as his nurse wheeled Looney to the front.

"Good looking out, you can bring her to my car." I handed him an envelope with his payment and left. I was going to get my ass back in the bed. "Looney, wake the fuck up!" I slapped her face a few times until she started stirring in her seat.

"Damn, Echo, I already got shot, how you gon' slap the shit out of me, too?"

It took everything in me not to laugh at the crazy look on her face. "I didn't even slap you hard. Come on so you can sleep this shit off and find out who tried to rob me tomorrow."

"Mothafuckas can't even get shot and recover in peace," Looney mumbled as she got out the car.

"Sure the hell can't, because if you would've been ready for shit like this, I wouldn't have been out my damn bed right now because you got a scratch," I countered. I ignored all the extra shit talking Looney was doing as I went to my bedroom.

When I got up the next morning, I was met with the little kicks of my babies. That was a relief since I was having that pain yesterday. I rolled out the bed and went to relieve my bladder they were tap dancing on.

"What the fu—oh no," I panicked as I looked at all the blood on the tissue and in the toilet.

"Good morning, babe."

"Na, I need help. Get over here, please." My heart was beating out my chest as I dragged myself out the bed.

"I'm on the way."

After I was dressed, I walked down to the front of the house to wait. I was met by Looney, who was already up and making calls. "You need to go see Wiz and see what she got. When you and Moe get this together, come see me at Christ."

"Everything a'ight?" Looney asked.

"What's wrong, Echo? What the hell happened to you?" Naomi rushed in the house and looked between me and Looney.

"I'm bleeding. We'll discuss the rest later." I stood and made my way out the house. Looney had keys to lock up, so I wasn't worried about that. I did pray all the way to the hospital for my babies, however.

3

NINA "LOONEY"

"HOW YOU FEELING, SISSY?" Wiz asked as I walked into her house.

"I'm breathing, so I'm good. Did you identify them bodies?"

"Yeah, they were some li'l niggas; nineteen years old." Wiz shook her head as she handed me the folders.

My phone rang, and it was Moe. "Yo, where you at?"

"Over here riding around the block, tryna see if somebody saw something. How you feeling over there?"

"I'm gucci. Meet me at Wiz's crib, we got to ride out somewhere."

"Bet, I'm 'bout to pull up," Moe said.

"Be careful out there," Wiz called out to my back as I walked upstairs. If anything, I was about to be even more alert. Ain't no way I was about to get caught lacking again.

I was standing outside when Moe pulled up, and I got right into the car. She gave me a quick look over, dapped me up, then backed out the driveway. "Who we going to see?" Moe asked as we came to a stop at the intersection.

I put the address in the GPS in the car and sat back. "We gotta deliver the sad news of their loved ones passing." Moe smiled as she followed the directions. That was what I loved about her: she never asked questions and was always ready to ride. The Big Man knew what He was doing when He made us, especially since we were born on the same day.

Twenty minutes later, we were pulling up to a house in Park Forest. I grabbed the extra gloves Moe had and put them on.

"Aye, Loon, we goin' in here with cool heads." Moe called herself giving me a pep talk as we walked up the few steps leading to the front door.

"I don't need you preachin' to me. I got this." I rang the doorbell and waited for someone to open the door.

"Hi, can I help you?" A middle-aged woman came to the door, and opened it enough to let us in.

"I'm looking for Colin. He hasn't answered his phone and I was a li'l worried," Moe said in a fake-ass concerned voice.

"I haven't seen him. Hold on. Chris!" She turned and screamed somebody's name. This nigga came limping around the corner, and when he saw us, all the color left his face. You could see it in his eyes he was going to run, and I was ready for it.

Click.

"If you run, I'ma make you scrape her brains off the wall," Moe warned as she pointed her gun to the woman's face.

"What the hell have you gotten into?" the woman cried.

"That's what we came to figure out. Come have a seat," I said, nodding towards a couch. We stayed standing against the wall so we could see everything around us. "So much for cool heads," I mumbled.

"Anybody else here?"

"No, my husband is at work. Look, I don't know what is going on, but please don't kill us." The woman who I assumed to be his mother begged for their lives.

"Why? Them niggas tried to kill me! I believe in an eye for an eye," I fumed.

"Ma, I swear I didn't know what we was going there to do." This nigga Chris started confessing his sins after just one look from his mama.

"Who was you riding with? And don't make me have to repeat myself because I will snatch all yo' fuckin' teeth out. Go." Moe pulled out some damn pliers from her pocket, and even I looked at her crazy. *How the fuck she tell me to be cool, but she came in here, pulling out tools and guns?*

"We ride with a nigga named Ghost. He don't stay too far from here, over in the Pangea Park Townhomes." This nigga was shaking so bad, I thought he was about to have a seizure.

"A'ight. Whatever yo' part in this is, you better continue on with business as usual. If this nigga gets a tip about anything we doing, I'm killing everybody you ever thought about loving." I looked this nigga in his eyes, so he knew I was serious.

"We'll see you around, Chris," Moe shouted on her way out the door. "So we going over there?"

"Just to watch for now. I'm about to have Wiz pull him up so we know who we looking for." I sent the text off to Wiz and, as always, she responded right away, saying she was on it.

"What you got planned in that head of yours?"

"You'll see. Just know that we gon' need an army." I smiled as my phone beeped and Wiz's name popped up.

Wiz: Don't make any moves sis. We all need to be involved.

Me: I got this, don't worry.

"This what the nigga look like." I showed Moe my phone and she nodded in approval.

"He's cute. Too bad he gotta die," Moe said laughing.

"We can wait until one of them other niggas come take over before we move around. Echo at Christ and we gotta fill her in."

"What the hell happened? Why you just now saying something?"

"Man, she told me to go handle business then come see her, so that's what I'm doing. If she wanted that shit broadcasted, she would've told you."

"You got it," Moe said, nodding.

"Yup." I didn't have time for Moe and her shit right now. My damn shoulder was starting to hurt, and I was ready to go lay up under my man.

4

MALIK "DETECTIVE STEVENS"

"Why are you fighting so hard to keep me away? I'm not going anywhere. Let me protect you from this shit."

"DETECTIVE STEVENS," I said into the phone as I drove home from another boring-ass day pushing paperwork.

"Hey, my name is Naomi. You don't know me, but I'm a friend of Echo's. I know she's probably not going to call you, but she's in the hospital."

"Is she okay? What happened? What hospital?" I rambled.

"She's at Christ," Naomi told me before hanging up.

I made a U-turn then headed to the hospital. When I pulled up, I had to flash my badge so they wouldn't try to have my car towed. I rushed to the front desk and had my badge out in case I had to show it again. "I'm looking for Echo Brady's room."

"Are you family, sir?" The front desk clerk looked me up and down like I smelled like shit.

"Yeah, that's my wife. Now where is her room?" I was getting frustrated and was ready to go to every floor, calling her name.

"I apologize, it's room 308," she finally told me. I snatched the pass that she was moving too slow to give to me and went to the elevator.

"We got people sitting there, Echo. Trust me on this one." I heard some hushed talking coming from inside her room, so I knocked to make myself known. There were six eyes staring back at me when I walked in.

"I'll call y'all later. Just keep eyes on everything for me," Echo said, dismissing them. Only one of them smiled at me, and I figured that was Naomi.

"Is everything okay? What happened?" The second the door closed, I started my questions.

"It was some bleeding, but they're okay." Echo just shrugged it off like it wasn't a big deal.

"Why was there bleeding? Stop fuckin' actin' like this isn't a big deal. Them my babies, too!" I yelled as I hit my chest. It was pissing me off that Echo was just lying there, looking at me like I was bothering her.

"Is everything okay in here?" some nosy-ass nurse poked her head in and asked.

"Yeah, everything is fine. I need a minute," Echo finally spoke. "Malik, I'm gon' let that slide because I understand you in your feelings. I should've called and let you know what was going on and that was my bad, but I got more pressing things to worry about."

"Like what? Whatever you were in here whispering about?"

"That's not your concern," Echo said dismissively.

"If it's affecting you and the safety of my babies, then it is my concern. How can I help?" I didn't know what the fuck I was saying, but just seeing Echo laid up in this hospital bed made me want to make sure they were protected. By any means necessary.

"Malik, just go. I can't have you in the middle of my mess again."

"Why are you fighting so hard to keep me away? I'm not going anywhere. Let me protect you from this shit."

"I don't fuckin' need help, Malik! I been watching my back my entire life, and I never needed a man to help me. That shit doesn't change just because I'm pregnant," Echo argued.

"But it should slow you down! Every move you make, you should be thinking if it's going to keep y'all safe."

"You hear that?" Echo asked as she touched a button on the machines next to her. I heard what sounded like some African drums beating. "They are safe. Don't ever think I would purposely put my babies in harm's way. You can go." Echo shooed me away like I was really about to leave.

I grabbed a chair from the corner and pulled it in at an angle, so I could get comfortable. "Like I said, I'm not going anywhere. I'll be here as long as you're here."

"Suit yourself." Echo could play that tough guy shit all she wanted, but I saw her smiling when she turned her head. I think I was finally starting to break her down.

∞

A RANDOM HOUR in the night

"HOW MANY MEN he got with him? Did you move my shit already? Call everybody and have 'em meet at Granny's house in an hour." Echo whispered on the phone, as I laid on this chaise, pretending to be asleep. Since Echo had been released from the hospital, I'd been staying at her house, making sure she stayed in bed.

For the first time, I'd used all the vacation days I had saved up from work. Once I knew Echo was in the clear, then I'd worry about work and shit. "Where do you think you going?" I spoke, scaring her.

"I got to handle something, and before you even speak, I won't be in danger." Echo walked to her closet and came back out with a Nike sweat suit.

"A'ight, I'm going, too." I stood up and stretched.

"Nah, I'm good, *detective*. You can stay right there until I get back." Echo chuckled as she got dressed.

"I'm just Malik right now. I'll leave my badge and gun here." Whether she liked it or not, I was following her wherever she was going.

"Well, you might need a gun. Just saying." Echo shrugged as she walked out the closet with two guns. She handed one to me and I looked at it. The serial number was missing, and I just had to shake my head.

"I'm not even gon' ask where you got this from," I said.

"Good, that's not something Malik would be asking about. We're taking my car," Echo announced.

I helped her into the passenger seat before I got behind the wheel. Echo showed me where to go, and twenty minutes later, I was pulling behind a ranch style home on 79th and Loomis. Echo led me through the back door, where some big, burly nigga opened the door for us. I walked down the hall in awe as I looked at the wall with all different types of guns lined up on it. From the outside, you wouldn't think this was in here. I rode past this house all the time and wouldn't even think to look twice at it. I guess that was the point.

"Have a seat, everyone should be here soon." Echo motioned for me to take a seat next to her, so I did. A few minutes later, all of the women I had seen in the hospital walked in the room. They all had mugs on their face.

"Okay, can we all address the pig in the room before everyone else shows up?" Looney asked with her hand raised.

"I think it's elephant, Looney," Moe laughed.

"Nah, G, it's definitely a pig."

"Cut the shit, Nina, Malik is here to help. Now, if you done actin' like a clown, we can address this shit for real." I was shocked to see Echo stand up for me. "With my pregnancy being high risk, I'm not going to be able to run out whenever. Moe and Looney, I need y'all to work as one to run this in my absence. I don't want to receive a call in the middle of the night about nothing. I also don't want to wake up to bodies on the news. Malik is here to act as extra security. This is not permanent. DB and Wiz, after tonight, you go back to your usual program."

"I got it," everybody chimed in at the same time.

I think I had really underestimated Echo and how powerful she was. There was at least twenty men standing in this room, following her every word. From what I gathered from this meeting, there was about to be a war. After she gave out demands, I sent Echo's ass home and I was going to ride out with them.

"The guys sitting outside of Ghost's spot said they're loading up now," Looney said, as she tapped away on her phone.

"This is the last time I'm going to ask. Are you sure you want to go along with this?" Echo stopped me from getting in the truck.

"I'm sure, now go home and I'll call you." I watched as Echo got in her car and left before I got in the truck. I was quiet as we rode a few blocks over to another building that looked abandoned.

"Everybody get in here and get in position. If we gon' shoot, we shoot to kill, remember that."

I felt like I was in the middle of a crazy-ass movie as I waited in the dark for some damn thugs to kick in the door and start shooting. My phone rang, and it reminded me that I had forgotten to call Echo. "What's up, baby? We waiting inside now."

"Keep the phone on so I can hear what's going on. They should be pulling up any minute."

"I see headlights!" someone called out.

My heart was beating fast as we waited in the shadows.

Boom!

The door flew open and the first round of people started marching in. "The house is empty, but I see some bags in the back."

"Pack that shit up and we'll torch this bitch," who I assumed was the ring leader instructed.

"Nah, you gon' leave that shit right there, right along with them guns." Looney and Moe came out first, followed by me and everyone else, pointing our guns at the group. "Now, lucky for you, Ghost, I decided to forgive you for shooting me, just like my boss is going to forgive you for thinking you were going to move in on what don't belong to you."

"I see it as open playing field. Ain't no way some bitches equipped to run this shit. Think of this as me helping you out," Ghost said with a smug look on his face.

Looney looked down at her phone, then smirked. "Is that your final answer?"

"Fuck you."

Pew!

"Oh shit!" I jumped back when a bullet whipped past me and hit Ghost in the middle of the head.

"Anybody else feeling like that, or you want to make some money?" Moe asked, looking them in the eyes. When no one moved, she smiled and clapped her hands. "Good choice. Get rid of this body. Do what you want to do with it."

"I'll see you when you get back to the house." Echo hung up and I just stood there, looking lost.

What the hell did I just witness?

5

ECHO "EJ"

LOONEY: You got twenty minutes until we make it to you.

I looked at the text and hurriedly packed my gun up and stuck it back in the compartment in my trunk. I hate that Malik was so predictable sometimes. Men, period. I knew he was going to jump in to be this big, bad man and keep me safe. I needed him to do that so I could keep my eyes on him. Instead of going home, I went to a secluded spot where I had the perfect view in my scope and waited. I was the one who put a hole in that nigga's head. He was going to die either way to set the tone for shit. Ghost was a warning to his people and anyone else who thought about messing with mine.

When Malik walked through the door, I was sitting on the couch, eating ice cream. "You supposed to be in the bed. And what I tell you about feeding my babies all this junk?" He flopped on the couch next to me and put my feet in his lap.

"Oh my Gooood, don't start right now. Can we just lay back and relax?"

"You need to be laying down, so we can relax in the bed." Malik picked me up while I held on to my bowl. After he laid me down, he stripped from his clothes and went to the bathroom.

My eyes went to his badge sitting on my dresser and I started to feel a little bad for the stuff I was putting him in. Then again, I wasn't forcing him to do anything and he was free to leave and do what he pleased.

"I think we should go stay at my place." Malik's voice brought me from my thoughts.

"Why would I do that?"

"Because I don't like the way yo' li'l boyfriend keep eyeing me when I come over."

"Who, Scott?" I busted out laughing. "You do not have to worry about Scott," I snickered.

"I didn't say I was worried, you just don't need this nigga running behind you no mo'." Malik had a scowl on his face as he put his boxers on.

"Awww, are you jealous, baby daddy?" I teased Malik and pinched his cheek.

"Man, move." Malik playfully pushed my legs off him and scooted over.

"I'm just joking. If you want me to go over to your house, then I'm fine with that." I laid my head on Malik's chest and he had an arm wrapped around me. "Thank you for having my back," I said sleepily.

"You don't have to thank me, it's my job." Malik placed a kiss on top of my head, then rubbed my back. It didn't take long for me to fall asleep in his arms.

The next morning, I woke up to breakfast in bed. While I sat and ate, Malik was packing up half my condo. I guess he was serious about me coming to his place. I didn't mind since it was closer to my doctor's office anyway. Walking into Malik's house gave a homey feeling. It felt like you were supposed to retire here. It had three bedrooms and two bathrooms. If he just updated some things, it would be perfect.

"You know you can go back to work whenever you want to. I don't need a babysitter," I said as I laid across Malik's king size bed.

"Damn, you tired of me already? Excuse me for enjoying this time with you."

"It's not that, but I know you bored in here, waiting on me hand and foot. I'm sure there's some bad guys that need to be caught," I joked.

"We'll see how your next doctor appointment goes before I decide that. So you stuck with me for a li'l bit longer."

"That don't sound too bad to me," I flirted and batted my eyes at him.

"You trouble, man, I swear." That was one thing I could agree with him on.

6

NADIA "WIZ"

"YO, WIZ!"

"I'm downstairs," I yelled back to Looney. I saw when she pulled up; I just thought she knew to come downstairs. If I was at home, then I was sitting in front of these screens. That was why my house stayed so clean.

"Yo' ass gon' be cockeyed sitting in front of that shit all day." I rolled my eyes at Looney as I turned to her. I was shocked to see she wasn't alone.

"Shut yo' ass up. How y'all doing?" I spoke to Moe and her brother as I stood to give her a hug.

"I'm tired from dealing with these two all day." Moe cut her eyes at Looney and Jay.

"I can only imagine. Now, what did I do to deserve this visit?" I knew it had to be something serious if they were meeting in person.

"We need to come up with another route to get shit here from Colombia," Looney spoke.

"This is where Jay comes in. He'll fly, and you direct. We need you to go on the first run to make sure he stays undetected," Moe countered.

"I don't know, man. You know I don't do good in the air. Why can't one of y'all go?"

"Don't tell me you scared to be alone with me, pretty?" Jay flirted as he reached for my hand.

I quickly snatched it back. "Not even a little bit. But you should be lucky what you put your hands on. I would hate for you to lose a hand."

"Ohhhh, feisty. And here I thought you was the nice one." Jay smirked at me.

"I'll do it, but only the first one. Give me a day and I'll have a route done."

"Thanks, sissy, I'll see you later." Looney hugged me, then threw up the deuces. I waved at them as they all made their way back upstairs.

I sighed as I turned my chair back to my computer. I pulled up a map and studied every route from here to Colombia. When deciding, I had to make sure we stayed off of DEA's radar when on the ground and in the air. If there were any mistakes, it could literally cost us everything. My ringing phone interrupted me, and I saw my mama's name pop up.

"What's going on, Nicole?"

"Is that how you answer the phone for the woman who birthed you?" she scoffed.

"Ma, I'm in the middle of something. Do you need something?"

"Well, I'm in the neighborhood and I wanted to stop by."

"In *my* neighborhood, for what?" My face was twisted up at that news.

"Don't question me, I'll be there shortly." My mama hung up before I could even say anything else. I really hated that I was the only one who kept in touch with my mama because she would pop up and guilt me into spending time with her.

I went upstairs and locked up the basement before she got here. It wasn't that I didn't trust Nicole, but she once stole everything we had of value for some drugs. I knew she was still using, no matter how much she tried telling me she'd stopped. I mean, it was our shit she was buying so I knew.

Ten minutes later, my doorbell rang, and I waited a few seconds before I opened the door. I smiled, but that instantly dropped when I saw her. My mother was a beautiful woman, so I was confused by the ashy looking woman standing in front of me with baggy clothes.

"You not gon' hug me?" she asked, looking hurt.

"Honestly, no, you need to come take a shower." I tried not to turn my nose up, but when I smelled her hair, I wanted to slap her.

"It's not that bad, Nadia. I'm trying the best I can." As always, she started with the waterworks, so I ushered her to the guest bathroom.

"Make sure you wash your hair a couple times," I called out. I heard her talking shit on the other side of the door, but I didn't care. I wanted to call Na and Looney, but I knew they wouldn't have cared. They had completely erased Nicole from their lives a long time ago. Me being the only one who always tried to help, she played on my love.

"That felt so good, thank you, baby." Nicole came out the bathroom wearing the clothes I had left in there for her. Her skin was glowing again, and her hair wasn't matted to her head anymore.

"Now, what did you come here for? Money?" I asked. I didn't want to waste any time with her pretending to care about what I'd been up to, or how much I made from the company.

"You don't have to be all nasty about it. That girl just turned you against me."

"That girl? You mean, Naomi, your daughter? She didn't do anything but pick up the slack for you. If it wasn't for Naomi, we would all be as lost as you." There was a lot I played about, but my sisters wasn't one of them.

"Look, I know I wasn't the best mother in the world, but I'm trying to make up now. I've been trying to get clean, and it's been a week now. That's why I came over here."

"You do know you're about twenty years too late? You always

come over here, singing the same song and you be right back doing the same stuff."

"Can you help me get into a program? I swear I'll stay there as long as I need to."

I sat staring in her eyes to see if I could read her or not. I'd lost count of how many times I'd helped her get into a rehab center, only for her to bolt. I didn't even think she was allowed back in any of the places in the city. Maybe it'd be good to get her away from the city. "If you can stay out of trouble for a few days, I'll have something together for you."

"Thank you, my sweet baby. How are your sisters doing?"

"They're good. Um, Na just had a baby, business is good, and Looney is still Looney," I shrugged.

"Na just had a baby?" Nicole shrieked. "I'm a grandma? Oh my goodness." Her face lit up, then dropped just as fast. "Is it a boy or girl?"

"A boy." I got my phone and showed her the pictures I had of Jamal Jr.

"Tell Naomi I said he's handsome." I noticed she tried to hurry up and swipe a tear away, so I just patted her back a little.

"Look, I have to be somewhere in a little bit and I still have some work to do."

"I get it, it's time for me to go."

"Here." I handed her two hundreds from my wallet and told her to take care. Hopefully, she was serious about getting clean this time. Like I said before, though, if I went through this only to get slapped in the face, I was wiping my hands of Nicole Richards.

7

NAOMI "NA"

"When the wrong people leave your life, the right things start happening."

YOU KNOW when you make a decision you really didn't think through until it was too late? That was me right now as I sat with Jamal, trying to come up with a schedule for JJ. That wasn't the bad part. My dumb mistake was having Looney and Moe here, playing mediator. We met at a lounge in Hyde Park because it was a neutral place. Looney was mugging Jamal so hard, I was just waiting for the guns to come out.

"Na, was this really necessary? We really got to sit down and have a damn custody battle?" Jamal asked me.

"That's if you choose to co-parent. If you choose to stay away, then that's cool, too."

"Don't play me like I'm a bum-ass nigga, G. You know I'm gon' take care of my seed regardless." Jamal's nostrils flared as he spoke, so I knew he was pissed.

"Well, Thursday through Saturday is for you, and we can switch off Sunday morning. Deal?"

"If that's what you really want to do," Jamal mumbled.

"Good, I'll see you in a few days." I stood from the table and headed towards the door. Looney and Moe were behind me and Jamal was still sitting.

"You should give me the green light to have him fucked up," Looney ranted as we walked through the parking lot.

"I don't need him dead. JJ still needs a father." I laughed at this fool.

"I didn't say I was gon' kill him, but he'll wish he was dead."

"No, Looney, we'll let karma handle him."

"Yeah, okay," she mumbled under her breath. I looked at Moe and she just threw her hands up, laughing. I already knew whatever Looney had planned, she was going to be right next to her. I learned many years ago not to waste my breath with my baby sister. She was going to do what she wanted.

We each got in our cars and went our separate ways. JJ was with Echo for the night, so I was spending the night catching up on stuff I needed at the restaurant. I had been handing off a lot of my work to my manager, and I needed to make sure I made the right decision. My restaurant was my first baby, and I would kill anyone who messed with it.

I stayed in my office all night. Well, I'd never left technically because I slept in the bed that was here. I turned off the do not disturb feature and watched as all the messages and missed calls popped up. Surprisingly, there weren't any from Echo. I just knew JJ was going to drive her crazy throughout the night. I ignored the text from Jamal and went to my contacts to call Echo.

"What do you want, stalker?" Echo answered on the first ring, and I could hear JJ babbling in the background.

"What's my baby doing? I know he miss me." I stood up from the bed and stretched.

"He's about three seconds from being sleep. Did you get a lot of work done last night?"

"Yeah, I did. I came up with a whole new menu and I'm ready to test it out."

"Good. Well, whenever you're ready to come get him, come on by. I'm about to try to nap with him because his little butt had me up at four in the morning," Echo yawned.

"Okay, well, when I get myself together, I'll be over." I got off the phone and went to the bathroom to get myself together. I took a quick shower, handled my hygiene, and threw on a Champion sweat suit. Once I was dressed, I packed up what I needed and left the office. I heard the chattering from my cooks in the kitchen, so I went to speak.

"Hey, ladies, let me get your attention real fast, I know you're busy." I waved my hand in the air to get everyone's attention.

"What's going on, boss lady?"

"I'm thinking about opening the club side more, so that means more hours for you all. I also have a new menu I want to try out. I'll probably put together a party and we can test it out then. Everybody okay with that so far?" I looked around the room and noted all the nods I received. "And don't worry, your pay will reflect your new responsibilities. You ladies have a good shift and call me if you need me." I left a few copies of the menu for them, then left.

Since I wanted to enjoy a little more alone time, I went to the mall to do some retail therapy. JJ had given me some extra hips I couldn't fit in my old jeans, so I needed to update my closet. I decided to go to Southlake Mall so I wouldn't see anybody I knew.

There were so many people walking around the mall, but I should've known it was going to be packed on a Saturday. All the fake ballers and card crackers were out, trying to stunt, and all the thirsty thots were trying to get chose. Then there was me, trying to get in and out without being seen.

"Excuse me, miss," I heard someone call out from behind me. I thought I was in the guy's way, so I scooted over a little. "Damn, you just gon' act like you didn't hear me, shorty?" Now that got my attention and I had to look back. When I did, I was looking up at a tall-ass basketball player looking dude.

"Excuse me?" I asked with my head tilted.

"I'm not trying to get kicked, I was just trying to get your attention." He licked his lips and flashed those extra bright white teeth.

"Okay, you got my attention now. So what?" I could tell by the shocked look on his face that he was used to women throwing themselves at him. I wasn't that woman, though.

"Let me start by introducing myself. I'm Cirmondo (Sir-mon-doh) but you can call me Monds," he said in a deep baritone voice. He held his massive hand out for me to shake, so I took it.

"Naomi," I introduced myself.

"Mmm, Naomi, it's definitely a pleasure to meet you. Now I'm gon' shoot straight from the hip and ask for your number. I know you don't know me, but I want to change that. Let me take you out sometime."

"That's nice, but I'm not really looking to date right now. I just got out of something, and it's really not the time." I gave him a half-smile and tried to move around to take the clutch and matching heels to the counter.

"How about we just go to lunch right now? Something tells me I'll be kicking myself if I just let you get away." I smiled at his smooth, corny butt before I agreed.

"Fine. If you're serious, then you'll meet me at Red Robins in an hour. If I have to wait for even a minute, then I'm leaving. If everything goes okay after this friendly lunch, then I'll think about giving you my number."

"That's not a problem for me, Queen. It's your world. I'll be there." Cirmondo took my hand and placed a kiss on it before going to the men's section.

I hid my smile as I put my items on the counter to check out. There was still another stop I wanted to make in the mall, so I went there before heading to Red Robins.

"Hi, welcome to Red Robins. How many in your party?" the host greeted me.

"I'm actually looking for someone I was supposed to be meeting." I scanned the small crowd in the restaurant and didn't see Cirmondo anywhere. I was a little disappointed because I was actually looking forward to something new.

"You must be Naomi. Your party is waiting right over here." The host shocked me by leading me to a secluded area. Cirmondo was sitting at a table that was covered in a white table cloth. "Enjoy."

"You are really trying to win some brownie points, I see," I said as Cirmondo pulled a chair out for me to sit.

"Yeah, why wouldn't I? I need to make sure I pass my test with flying colors. How am I doing so far?"

"So far so good."

I was like a school girl the way I was smiling and giggling all throughout this lunch. The conversation with us flowed so perfectly, and I felt like I'd known him for years. Being on this date made me realize that was where me and Jamal had gone wrong: we forgot to take time out just for us after a while. I was making sure I never found myself in that situation again.

"So, Miss Naomi, do I get the privilege of exchanging numbers with you?" Cirmondo asked as he walked me out to my car.

"I gueeesssss I can give you my number since you fed me and all," I joked.

"I'll take that win any way I can." We switched phones and locked each other in. Like the gentleman he was, Cirmondo helped me into the car. "I'll be seeing you again soon," Cirmondo noted as he placed a kiss on my hands.

I smiled and waved as I pulled out the lot. "I still got it," I said aloud to myself as I headed to Malik's house where Echo was. I knew the girls weren't going to believe this.

8

ECHO "EJ"

"It's okay to be scared. The way things have been going, you should be."

"THANK you so much for watching him for me, bestie," Naomi thanked me for the hundredth time as she was leaving with JJ.

"Whenever you want us to watch him again, it's not a problem," Malik spoke before I could.

Naomi made a silly look at me as she headed down the steps. "I'll be sure to keep that in mind. Bye, guys."

"Let me know when you make it in," I called out. "How are you gon' just volunteer me to do something?" I asked Malik once he closed and locked the door.

"My bad, I guess I got a little carried away. How could you not want to keep him, though? That's a handsome dude and he's such a good baby. I hope we get lucky like that." Malik smiled from ear to ear like he always did when he talked about babies.

"Well, trust, I'm not in a rush to be dealing with that times two.

The peace and quiet we hear right now will all be a thing of the past in a few short months. I can only imagine how I'll deal alone." I shook my head.

"Why would you be doing it alone?" Malik looked at me like I had sprouted a few extra heads.

"When I go home, Malik. I'm not crazy enough to think this situation is permanent. I know once the babies get here, we'll have to get settled into my place."

"I'm not even going to respond to that. You about to ruin this day already," Malik mumbled as he left me sitting in the front by myself.

I sat on the couch for a while to see if he was going to come back. After twenty minutes, I figured he was mad for real and went to find him. "What's the problem, Leaky?" I was trying to joke to lighten the mood and it didn't work.

"I really need to know what's the problem. I been breaking my neck to try to prove that we'll be good together, and you still fighting me. We're about to bring two babies into this world and you're handling me like I'm just a random nigga helping you out."

"You're being a little dramatic, Malik. All because I said I was going home after the twins are born? We're not together, Malik."

"Because of some shit you got with you! I been told you I want you and this family we building. I ain't talked to my own damn family because I picked you over their bullshit. I'm a real man trying to step up and do this right. You need to stop pushing me away before I be gone for real." Malik's words stung my heart a little bit, but I still held my stone-cold face.

"I never asked you to do the things you're doing. I don't know what you want from me, but I don't know if I can give that to you."

"I just want your heart. Let me love you, Echo." Malik's voice softened as he made his way to me. He wrapped one hand around my waist, bringing me closer to him and rubbed my stomach with the other.

"I'm scared," I admitted. "I can't be weak in this world, and when I'm near you, I feel weak."

"You not, you're far from weak. You're one of the strongest women I've ever met, and I admire that about you. I know you don't need me and that makes me want you more. Stop fighting me, Echo," Malik whispered close to my ear, sending shocks through my body.

I looked up into Malik's big, brown eyes and I wanted to believe everything he'd ever told me. "Okay, I'm done fighting," I finally said to him. Malik moved closer to me and kissed me deeply. I felt my knees get weak and he had to hold me up. I couldn't have any type of sex and I was fiending for it right now.

"I know what you thinking, and I promise once you're cleared, I'ma fuck you all night. Don't worry, mama." I giggled when Malik slapped my ass and grabbed a handful of it. It seemed like I was carrying my babies in my ass because that was almost sticking out as far as my belly was. That was one thing I hoped to keep at least half of after I had them.

¢

"Damn, is this a gender reveal or a concert?" Malik asked as we pulled up to Rich Dreams.

"Me and my family believe in go big or go home. We work hard so we can celebrate even harder," I explained shortly. He'd soon see that whenever we decided to have a party, expect everything to be over the top.

"Yeah, I see." Malik parked at the gold carpet that was laid out. He helped me out and we posed to take some pictures.

"The guests of honor are finally here," Naomi announced over the microphone. There had to be about seventy people in the room. Most were business partners who I'd grown close to, and others were family and friends. None of Malik's family had come, or were even invited, except for Malani. She would always be my little sister.

"Ayo, E!" I heard behind me. I turned to see my guy Zo and his wife walking towards me.

"Hey, Yemani boo, you look so cute." I hugged her and eyed her small baby bump. "What's going on, Zo?" I gave him a hug next.

"Ain't shit, you know me. When I got that invite, I thought this shit was a joke. Maaan, you about to have two. Ye, after you pop this one out, we gotta try for triplets. I know my soldiers strong enough for it."

"Deronzo, stop it." Yemani's face turned red as she swatted at Zo.

"Anyways, this is Malik, my guy. Malik, this is Zo and his wife, Yemani." I introduced them.

"How you doing, man?" Malik held his hand out, and Zo just gave Malik a blank stare. The way he was staring at Malik, it was like he was reading his life story. I started to get nervous, thinking I was going to have to shoot Zo's ass until Yemani nudged him.

"I got a thing with germs, but what's good?" Zo gave him a head nod, and I just shook my head. "Congratulations, y'all. E, come holla at me before the night over," Zo said, then grabbed Yemani's hand to lead her away.

"Guess he knows I'm a detective," Malik said, laughing.

"Zo is just extra careful about those around him. Don't worry about that. I'm ready to get a plate, though." I quickly changed the subject, then walked to the table in the middle of the room. After I stuffed my face, Naomi came out, announcing that it was time for the reveal. We had done the ultrasound last week, and I was going crazy waiting for the results.

"So I know you wanted to keep it simple so all y'all have to do is pull the string and the confetti will show what the babies are." DB handed me and Malik our cannons and stood back.

"On the count of three! One... two... three..."

I pulled my string and saw all the pink confetti flying out. I looked over at Malik and his cannon was full of blue confetti. He hugged me so tight, I had to hit his chest to let me go.

"Thank you," Malik said over and over as he kissed me.

"Okay, y'all, damn, back up and breathe," Looney's hating ass said.

"Congrats, you guys. I can't wait until my little niece and nephew get here," Malani gushed. He hugged me and Malik tight before stepping back.

The rest of the party, we ate and listened to music. It was good being in a room filled with so much love. I was happy to see my mama there, especially. She wouldn't stop crying when she saw what the babies were. The one thing I knew, these babies were surrounded by love already.

As the party started to wind down, I remembered Zo wanted me, so I pulled him away from Yemani for a second. I led him to the hall where we had a quiet place to speak freely. "What's up, Zo?"

"What's up with ya mans? You in deep, huh?" Zo asked, leaning against the wall with his arms crossed.

"He's cool, trust me. That's not the problem I'm having, though," I explained.

"What's up, baby sis?"

"There's some people planning some attacks on my territory because they think we're out of business. I already had to clean one mess up, but I can't afford to keep handling it."

"Whatever you need from me, let me know."

"I just need some extra men, at least for the next couple months. I'll pay for whatever housing expenses while they're here."

"You good, we family. I'll send some cats down here. Who in charge while you baking them babies?"

"Looney and Moe."

Zo whistled and laughed a little. "Shit, you don't need my soldiers. I'm surprised everybody ain't dead yet."

"Man, I've been working with them on self-control. It's a struggle." I shook my head.

"All bullshit aside, you know I got you for whatever. I'll have some men here by tomorrow morning. You just worry about bringing them babies into the world."

"Thank you, Zo." I gave him a hug before he got ready to leave. We had to get a van to move all the gifts from the club to our place. There was so much shit in there, I think I'm going to have to get some walls torn down in their nursery for everything.

My feet looked like two pillows by the time we got in and I had to hear Malik's mouth about not leaving the bed for a week. I blocked all that out because the excitement I had from my babies outweighed it all.

9

MALIK "DETECTIVE STEVENS"

"For me, family always comes first. I would do anything to protect them." -Mark Wahlberg

AFTER WEEKS of being in the house, I finally decided to go back to work. The second I walked in, I was met with a stack of folders on my desk from a new case I was being assigned to. Ever since that case with Echo flopped, I had been begging for a case, but I was getting black balled every time. I thought it was my dad pulling the strings at first because I refused to talk to him. Until he let go of the grudge he had against Echo, I wouldn't be around.

"Hey, Detective Stevens, welcome back. How was your vacation?" One of my coworkers poked her head in my office seconds after I walked in. The main reason I wanted this office was because I finally had a door for privacy after being in those cubicles. The door was open, so I couldn't really be too mad.

"Thank you, it was well needed."

"I hear that." She nodded in agreeance and just stood there, looking like she had something else to say.

"Can I help you with something?" I finally asked.

She took a step closer like she had been waiting for me to say that. "I was wondering if you wanted to go out for some drinks or something sometime." Shocked wasn't even the word to describe how I felt. Don't get me wrong, Detective Tatum is beautiful, but since me and Echo were finally official again, I wasn't trying to mess that up. Especially being who she is.

"Uhh, I'm sorry, I can't do that. I'm in a relationship." Her face fell from the smile she had, and I started to feel bad.

"I understand, have a good day." Tatum slowly backed out of my office. That was a nice way to start the work day.

I flipped open the first file on my desk and read about a low-level drug dealer who had made enough noise to get our attention. From the information gathered already, he was connected to a few overdoses that had happened a few weeks ago. I knew I shouldn't have, but I took a picture of his mugshot with my phone, then looked at the other evidence. When it was time for me to leave for break, I decided to shut down and just take the rest of the day off.

"Hey, what you doing here?" Echo asked as I walked into the house and threw my stuff down. She was laying across the sectional and I came and sat next to her.

"I live here, what you mean?" I played dumb as I loosened my tie.

"You know what I meant," Echo said with attitude.

"It's my lunch time, but I decided to call it one. Let me ask you something, though." I pulled my phone out. "Do you know this dude?" I showed her the picture and she looked for a minute before shaking her head.

"Nah, don't look familiar. Who is he?" Echo asked, looking up at me. It was like she knew I was going to try to read her and see if she was lying or not.

"I was assigned this case because he's supposed to be responsible for some dirty coke that's going around the city."

"Oh, yeah?" Echo stared straight ahead at the TV, but I could tell she wasn't paying attention to what was on it. "Malik, are you going to get your phone while you're staring a hole in my head." Echo snapped me from my trance and I held my phone up. I saw my parents' house phone number pop up and I sighed.

"Yeah," I answered the phone dryly.

"Yeah? I know if I don't see you before I close my eyes, that'll be there when you open yours." Hearing my mama threaten me, I chuckled.

"I love you, too, Ma. I'll be there in a little bit."

"Mmmhhmmm." She hung up while I was still laughing.

"I guess I'll see you later." Echo's voice was filled with humor as she looked over at me.

"You got jokes, I see. But yeah, I'll see you later when I leave from there." I gave Echo a few pecks before leaving back out. Mid-day traffic getting to my parents' house was terrible. The entire ride, I hoped this wouldn't turn into her trying to preach to me about my Pops. I knew he hadn't told her why we were at each other's neck, and that was for the best.

"I just knew I was going to have to come out and find you." My mama gave me a smile and hugged me tight when she opened the door.

"I'm sorry, Ma. I ain't mean to be missing in action like that," I apologized. "How you been?"

"Getting old, shit, and tired of chasing behind my grown children. How's Echo?" My mama was chatting as she led me to the kitchen and went back to busying herself at the stove. I sat at the dining table and waited for the food.

"She's doing good, on bed rest right now, but they're okay. We're having a boy and a girl." I smiled big, thinking about my seeds growing.

"I don't see how you and Junior are popping out these twins. We're going to have a full house for Christmas now." My mama smiled big and I already knew it was because she was proud of being a grandmother.

"I'm thinking about proposing to Echo," I blurted.

"That would be so beautiful, Leaky. I can tell you really love her." I thought about what my mama had just said and that was the truth. The way I'd been risking my life, freedom, and career for her without a blink told me all I needed to know.

"What would be beautiful? It's nice to see you finally came to your senses." My Pops walked in the kitchen and kissed my mama on the cheek before turning to me.

"Let me get out of here." I stood up, but my ma stopped me.

"I don't know what is going on, but you two better cut the shit now. Life is too short for you two to be bickering about whatever pissing contest is going on. Fix it, Martin!" She turned the fire off on the stove and threw her apron on the counter.

"Look, it ain't much for us to talk about. We both got secrets. Your hands aren't clean in this situation while you're trying to paint this fucked-up picture of Echo," I pointed out.

"You're right, but if I wouldn't have agreed to her terms, she would've had me killed and got the next person to agree to her terms. I don't want you getting yourself in something you can't get out of, all in the name of love."

"Well, it's too late for that. No matter what, she is going to be the mother of my kids and my wife if she accepts. Whether you choose to be there or not is up to you." I stood, looking my dad straight in the eyes. There were a few moments of silence before he spoke.

"If you're serious about this, then I will support you. I don't agree fully, but you're my son and sometimes you have to learn lessons yourself. Just remember that people like Echo and her associates aren't people you can trust one hundred percent. If you're going to be with her, protect yourself first at all times."

"I appreciate that, Pops." He pulled me into a quick hug just as my mama was coming back. She had her hands on her hips as she looked back and forth.

"Is everything okay now?" she asked.

"Yes, ma'am," I spoke.

"Good, now come set this table." For the first time in damn near a month, I sat down and enjoyed a meal with my parents. I texted Echo to see if she wanted me to bring her a plate and she told me yeah and that she was getting ready to get some rest. I decided to stay and play catch up once Malani showed up, too. We were right back to being the fake Huxtables again.

10

ECHO "EJ"

"For every life lost, there's a life gained."

BREATHE, EJ...*breathe,* I coached myself in my head as I stared at the picture of this duck-ass nigga Prime that Malik was showing me. Prime was a li'l nigga who used to cop from me. I say used to cop from me because this nigga was about to die. The number one rule for doing business with me is Do. Not. Step. On. My. Shit. That shit is punishable by death, and clearly this nigga thought it was a joke. When Malik's mom called him, I had to send a quick 'thank you' up to the Big Man. I rushed to the room as fast as my belly would allow and grabbed my phone.

"Wassup, Boss Lady? Shouldn't you be somewhere with your feet up?" Looney joked when she answered the phone.

"Get word out that we need to have a round table discussion. We got a problem with niggas not keeping their feet off my lawn," I spoke in code. Even though my case was dropping, I couldn't chance that these niggas were still watching me.

"Say no more." Looney hung up and I slipped my feet into some Crocs. I knew I was going to get clowned but these were the only shoes that were comfortable right now.

Malik: Ma cooked, you want me to bring you a plate?

Seeing Malik's text made me remember that I had to think of something to tell him in case he made it back before me.

Me: Yeah, I'll probably be sleep when you get in. I'll see you when you get back.

I sent the text, then left out the house.

"Nice to see you again, Ms. Brady." My driver greeted me with a smile, then helped me inside.

"I told you to just call me Echo. How's the family?" Benson had been my driver for about as long as I had been in the game. He'd literally watched me grow over the years. I trusted him with my life.

"You know Sheree is still her crazy self. I see you're starting a family of your own. Congratulations."

"Thank you. God wanted to humor the world and blessed me with two." I rubbed circles on my stomach as I spoke. "Take me to Dearborn," I told him. We were just sitting in front of the house and I wanted to hurry up and get this over with.

We pulled up to Dearborn Meats, and Benson pulled through the gangway. "Stay close," was all I said before getting out. I noticed the girls' cars parked and were glad they had made it first so I could fill them in. Using my key to let me in the back door, I got in the elevator and went down to the basement. The meat market was just one of the many places I used to stash whatever I wanted. Also, when I had meetings like today, I used it because I had tools on hand in case I needed it. Like I knew I would today.

"Where's your guard pig?" Looney asked, making everyone laugh, except for me.

I took my seat and ignored her. "We're here because a nigga broke the law. It's a lot of shit I play about, and my name isn't one of them."

"Bro, I ain't never seen yo' ass play about shit," Looney interrupted me.

"Would you like to leave and take this comedy show on the road? Because I don't have time for this shit right now," I snapped.

"My bad, G." Looney threw her hands up and sat back in her seat. "Babies got her cranky as fuck," she mumbled.

"Like I was saying, a nigga broke the law and we're here to be the judge, jury, and executioner."

"Damn it, EJ, I just did my nails," DB complained as she looked down at her hand. I just shrugged and waited for everybody else to show up. Twenty minutes later, the room was filled with all of my lieutenants, as well as any nigga who I sold to in the area.

"Cellphones and weapons in the bin, you know the deal." Wiz and DB rolled the bins around and everyone followed directions. I waited until everything was put away before I spoke.

"What was one of the first things I said to each and every one of you before we even started making money? Prime." When I called him out, my girls knew he was the one who had fucked up.

"U-uh, you said a lot," he chuckled nervously.

"What's rule number one?"

"Don't step on the product." Moe answered for him. I stood up and had a lot of shocked eyes on my swollen belly.

"Spread out." At my command, all the men in the room stood up and moved their chairs. "Prime, step up. Before you even try to think of a lie, let me tell you how dumb you are. Whatever shit you was mixing is killing these junkies out there. There's an open investigation on you."

"EJ, let me explain. Shit's been tight. I-I got a baby on the way and I needed to help my OG out." This nigga was pouring so many excuses out his ass, it didn't make any sense.

"If there was ever a problem any one of you had financially, you could've easily came to one of us. We make sure everyone eats in this camp, right?" I yelled in his face. "Bring me my bag."

Prime's eyes got big as I opened up my black bag and took out all my torture pieces. I pulled stuff out until I found what I was looking for. "Are you right handed or left handed? Don't matter, hold 'em both out."

"EJ, please, you don't have to do this. Ahh!" I took my mallet down across his knuckles and Prime screamed like he was trying to give Mariah Carey a run for her money with those high notes. Once I was sure every finger was broken on both hands, I stopped.

"Put him out of his misery. Let this be a reminder to all of you what will happen if you think of fuckin' with my shit. You may go." I watched the men grab their belongings before leaving.

"I already called cleanup," Wiz announced.

"Tell them to drop him somewhere his family will find him. I'm not that fucked up." I laughed, which was cut short by a sharp pain in my abdomen. "Ooww, shit," I cursed as I doubled over in pain.

"What happened?" The girls rushed to me and started grabbing on me before I lost my balance.

"I don't know—ooww! Take me to the hospital, please!" I screamed at the top of my lungs as another pain crippled me.

"Shit, y'all help me carry her to my truck. Then y'all make sure this shit gets cleaned up." Naomi threw out demands as she rushed out the door.

When I was laid across her backseat, the pain subsided, and I was able to catch my breath. "Please don't let me be losing my babies. This my karma for sneaking out," I cried hysterically.

"Echo, baby, I need you to calm down before you raise your pressure through the roof and make it worse. Everything's going to be okay. Maybe you should call Malik, so he can get to the hospital."

"Okay," I sniffled, grabbing my phone. I took a deep breath before I hit Malik's contact.

"You must've changed your mind about the food." Malik answered the phone, laughing.

"No, you need to—ooowww!" The pain came back, stopping my sentence.

"What happened, you okay?" I could hear the panic in his voice.

"Meet me at the hospital." I hung up and focused on breathing. We finally made it to the hospital and Na pulled up to the door.

"Let me go get somebody." Naomi hopped out and ran inside. She came back seconds later with three nurses and a security guard.

"Hi, ma'am, what's your name?" The nurse spoke as they helped me into the wheelchair.

"Echo Brady."

"What's going on, Echo?"

"I'm in pain, and I need to make sure my babies are okay."

"On a scale of one to ten, what do you rate the pain?"

"Ten!" I screamed as the pain and pressure came back. They wheeled me up to a room and had me change into a gown. I saw the blood in my panties and froze. "I'm bleeding!"

The nurse ran to me and helped me in the bed. I laid back while she put the monitors across my stomach. It took her a while to find their heartbeats and I was ready to cry. "Here they are," the nurse announced. I let out a deep breath and tried to relax.

"Good afternoon, Echo. I'm Dr. Terry, the doctor on call. I reached out to your doctor and he should be on the way. I'm just going to take a look at what's going on." Dr. Terry washed her hands and grabbed the ultrasound machine. She put the cold gel on my stomach and the second the probe touched me, I was in pain again.

"Wait, wait." I stopped her from touching me until the pain was gone.

"How often have you had that pain?" Dr. Terry asked.

"It's been every couple of minutes. I couldn't really time it, but it's the second since I've been here."

"Well, it definitely looks like labor, but my concern is the babies. Not only are you only thirty-three weeks, the babies are not responding well to the contractions, and it's causing their heart rates to drop." She looked over the papers the nurse handed her and nodded. "I'm going to have them give you some pain medication through an IV so you can be comfortable. If you need anything, hit the button."

"Thank you." Dr. Terry and the nurse left out and Naomi and Malik walked in shortly after.

"What are they saying?" Malik looked stressed as he approached me.

"I'm in labor but the babies are in distress after every contraction," I summed it up.

"What are they going to do?" Naomi had tears in her eyes.

"Well, they're about to give me something for the pain and I'll see when my doctor gets here." I had another contraction that was worse than any one I'd ever had. The machine next to me started beeping like crazy, and all of a sudden, my room was filled with nurses and Dr. Terry.

"We need to get the babies out of there, Echo, I just need your permission." Dr. Terry was talking to me as the nurses propped me to lay on my left side. It felt like everything was moving too fast.

"Echo." Malik's voice snapped me from my trance.

"Okay, let's do it." The second I agreed, I was whisked off to an operating room. Only one person could be with me, so, of course, it was Malik. As I sat getting this anesthesia, I hated every minute of it. I felt like I had failed because I couldn't carry my babies full term or deliver them naturally."

"Echo, we're going to be starting now. How are you feeling?" Dr. terry asked from over the sheet that was blocking everything from the boobs down.

"I'm okay." My voice was so soft, I didn't recognize it. Malik was led into the room and to a chair that was by my head.

"Just relax, it's going to be okay," Malik whispered in my ear. He kissed me, and I felt my body relax. The epidural had definitely kicked in and I didn't feel anything going on beyond that little sheet.

After minutes of waiting, I felt some tugging. "Okay, we have baby A out, and it is a boy." Dr. Terry handed the baby off to a nurse, and then three nurses followed her to the incubator.

"Why isn't he crying? Malik, go check on him." I started hyperventilating and.

"Calm down, I'll go check." Malik stood up and walked to the side of the room where the baby was. *Oh my God, we don't even have names for our babies.*

"Okay, Mom, here's baby B. It's a girl." This time, I heard little cries and I started crying. I knew that probably meant we were going to have trouble with that one. Forty minutes later, I was cleaned up and put into my private suite where I was going to be recovering. Me and the twins had an entire wing to ourselves. When I decided to have my babies at Christ, I paid for them to build a suite that could act as a NICU if needed. I didn't want to be away from my babies.

I couldn't hold them yet because they had to stay in the warmer a little longer than normal. Our baby boy weighed three pounds, fifteen ounces and was twenty inches long. Our crybaby girl weighed four pounds, nine ounces and was twenty inches long. I guess she was bossing him around in the wound and taking his food.

"Man, what are we going to name them?" Malik asked as he laid in the bed with me.

"I was thinking that earlier," I giggled. "Are you one of those guys who just needs to have a junior?"

"Nah, I mean, it'll be nice, but it's not like I need it."

"Okay, good, because that wasn't happening. My son needs his own identity."

"You do know he's a twin, right?"

"Malik, shut up." I punched his arm playfully. I laid in his arms and we both watched the babies. They were laying together, and you could notice the weight difference between the two. They both were still so tiny. Baby Boy was hooked up to a machine, helping him breathe. Besides that, they were healthy. To be preemie twins, I was blessed that they were doing so well.

Staring at my babies, I couldn't understand how anyone could leave their child voluntarily. I knew it wouldn't be a cake walk, especially with two of them, but only death could make me leave them.

∞

After the first three days of being in the hospital, I was starting to go crazy. The pain I was in from this c-section was no joke. Then, I kept spiking fevers, so I was forced to stay longer. The only good thing from all this was my babies, who, in fact, still didn't have names. Baby Boy was still on a machine helping him breathe, and he also had a feeding tube. Meanwhile, Baby Girl was fine, the doctors just needed her to gain two pounds before they could talk about discharging her. I attempted to breastfeed her, and the shit was painful because this little girl was greedy.

Knock. Knock.

"Come in," I called out as I put my boob back up. My ma walked in and she was all smiles.

"How are my babies doing?" Ma asked as she washed her hands. I already knew she was coming for my baby, so I handed her over.

"We're good, ready to go home," I expressed.

"Well, you and these babies' health are what's important, so you better not be giving these people a hard time for doing their job," my mama fussed. "Where's Malik?"

"I told him to go back to work. There's no need for us both to be prisoner here."

"Well, I hope you're taking it easy. That was a serious surgery you had, Echo."

"I know, Ma," I groaned. No matter how old I got, my mama would fuss at me like I was that same bad ass Echo from when she first got me.

"I'm just trying to make sure you're okay. Now, did y'all name my grandbabies yet? I can't even brag about them right just calling them him and her." I laughed because this lady was crazy.

"Not yet, but I know they'll have one before they leave here."

"What the hell are y'all waiting for? You know what, I'll give them my own names." I always missed my mama until she started trying to take over something. She did show me how to get Baby Girl to properly latch on so it wasn't painful to feed her.

I know it sounds bad, but I was happy when Liz came to pick her up. Not only was she getting on my nerves after the first hour, I was ready to take a nap.

The sun had just gone down when Malik came back to the hospital. He looked dead tired but still tended to the twins until he fell asleep. He actually fell asleep rocking Baby Girl and I had to get her and lay her in her bed.

My business phone rang, and I knew it was going to be some shit.

"Speak."

"The truck never made it and the driver is in the wind." Hearing that had my blood boiling.

"How the fuck does a whole ass truck disappear? Go find my fuckin' truck and that driver. Pay his family a visit, somebody knows something." I hung up and slammed my phone down on the sink. Niggas wanted to test me when I was down like this was permanent. When I got my hands on whoever the fuck it was, motherfuckers were going to see the beast I tried to keep hidden.

11

MALIK "DETECTIVE STEVENS"

I HEARD a loud banging noise and jumped up from the slumber I was in. I frantically looked on the floor for my baby girl, praying I hadn't dropped her.

"What are you looking for?" Echo came out the bathroom with her phone clutched tightly in her hands.

"Shit, I thought I dropped the baby. Everything okay with you?" I could tell something was bothering her from the look on her face.

"Nothing. I'm glad you're up, though." Echo climbed in the bed and I got in behind her once I undressed.

"What's going on?" I carefully pulled Echo to me so she could lay on my chest.

"We need to name the babies before it's time to go home."

"That's funny you saying that now because I was thinking the same thing. Since you said I can't have my junior, do you have an idea of what you want their names to be?"

"I've always liked the name Elijah."

"I like that. Elijah Malik, right?"

"Fine, Malik, you're really determined," Echo giggled.

Echo and I stayed up talking and trying to come up with a name for Baby Girl. Echo kept saying she wanted Baby Girl's name to be something strong. Before we dozed off, we decided that Eva Meghan was a good fit for her.

The next morning, I woke up to my phone blowing up. I didn't know what was going on, but my ma was calling me back to back.

"Malik, I just got her back to sleep, you better get that phone," Echo fussed, then popped me in the back of the head.

"Damn, man. Hello," I groaned into the phone.

"My grandbabies were born, and I have to find out through your sister?" My mama was screaming so loud, I had to pull the phone back.

"Ma, calm down, it's too early to be yelling." I sat up in the bed and noticed Echo was dressed in leggings and a tank. Before I could ask her where she was going, my mama was back tearing into my ass.

"Oh, it's too early to be yelling, huh? Just wait until I get up to that hospital." The phone went quiet and I checked the screen to see she had hung up on me.

"What was that about?" Echo asked me.

"I think I'm about to get a whooping." Both me and Echo died laughing after I told her what had just happened. "She said she was on her way, so let me get up just in case. You headed out?"

"Not really. I got to go handle something minor."

"Echo, you just gave birth and got a million stitches in your abdomen. Don't you think you need to take a break and let somebody else handle your *business?*"

"I'm just going down the hall to have a private conversation with my sister. The babies are gone to get some test ran and should be back in a minute." And with that, Echo switched her ass out the room. She was moving around like she hadn't just gotten cut open a few days ago. If she kept that up, she was going to find herself staying in this hospital longer.

While I had this time alone, I went to shower and handle my hygiene. It felt like the last few weeks I had been running around in a twilight zone. If I wasn't worried about Echo and the pregnancy, I was worried about Echo and her choice of career. Crazy thing is, I hadn't heard Echo talk about opening *The Gallery,* let alone picking up a paint brush. I would hate for her talent to go to waste because she would rather chase these dope girl dreams.

"Are you sure this is where they told us to go?" I heard Malani's voice on the other side of the bathroom door.

"It better be. I'm not about to be running all over this hospital," my mama countered.

"How are two of my favorite ladies doing today?" I finally made myself known. I hugged my ma and gave her a kiss on the forehead while she mean mugged me the whole time.

"Where's Echo and the babies?" Malani asked, then looked around the spacious suite.

"They should be back here any minute, but here's some pictures." I handed them my phone and they huddled together.

"Aawww, look at them. They're so tiny and precious. What did you guys name them?" My ma wiped tears from her eyes.

"Elijah Malik Stevens, and Eva Malika Stevens," I said with my chest poked out.

"You could've named my niece after me," Lani joked. We all laughed, but it was cut short when the door flew open. Echo stomped into the room with a perplexed look on her face.

"Well, hello, Echo," my mama spoke, snapping Echo from whatever trance she was in.

"Hey, Mrs. Stevens, when did you all get here?" Echo smiled, but I could tell it was fake. Whatever went on with Naomi must be bad.

"We just got here not too long ago, waiting on those babies."
Knock. Knock.

"Hiiii, we're just here to bring these two bundles back. They both passed their hearing test with flying colors. The doctor will be in here shortly to discuss some things with you two," the nurse informed us before leaving.

"Ooohhh, Ma, look," Malani cooed as they stood over the twins.

Echo took that time to sneak off to the bathroom, so I followed her. "I need a minute."

"We got a minute, so tell me what's going on," I demanded. "The truth."

Echo sighed before answering me. "I got word that one of my shipments went ghost. That's three million dollars I can't afford to lose, no matter how much money I have in the bank."

"Three million fuckin' dollars, Echo?" I whispered harshly. I didn't want my nosy mama or sister hearing what was going on.

"Yes! And I need to get that shit back before—ooww!" Echo bent over, holding her stomach.

"You need to go lie down, come on."

"I'm fine." I ignored her, picked her up bridal style, and carried her to the bed. "You're doing the most right now."

"Save that attitude shit. I'm here to help you, not hurt you, remember that. You need to rest, and when we leave here, then *we*," I said, waving my finger between us, "will figure this out together. Got it?"

"Yeah." Echo gave me a smirk and I saw the lust in her eyes. The way I felt, when Echo was cleared to have sex again, I might fuck around and put two more babies up in her.

"Ahem." My mama clearing her throat got our attention. She was holding Eva and standing a few feet away from us. "If you two are done eye sexing each other, I think she's hungry." Eva was trying to peck away at my mama's shirt.

"I'm not surprised, she's always hungry." Echo laughed and grabbed Eva from my mama. Echo whipped her breast out to feed Eva like it was nothing.

"We're going to get out of your hair. I will be back to see you all soon when you go home. I need to hold my grandson over there so he can know me."

"Okay, Ma, y'all be careful and let me know when you make it in."

"Take care of them, Malik. All of them." Malani gave me a stern look before following behind my mama.

That's not something I needed somebody to tell me. No matter what I was going to take care of my family, and I already knew where I was going to start.

12

NAOMI "NA"

"The axe forgets, but the tree remembers." -African proverb

A FEW WEEKS later

KNOCK. Knock.

"I'm coming!" I sat JJ in his playpen, then opened the door for Jamal. He called saying he wanted to see JJ, so I invited him over. I knew it was just his way of trying to ease his way in, but I figured I'd see what he wanted. I opened the door and Jamal was standing there with flowers and cashew turtles.

"You're looking good, Na," Jamal complimented, handing me the stuff in his hand.

"Yeah, I know." I locked the door behind him and walked to the living room. He picked JJ up and his eyes lit up as he looked up at Jamal.

"Listen, I wanted to talk to you without arguing. Can we do that?"

"Just say what you have to say, Jamal." I opened my turtles and grabbed one.

"That baby isn't mine. My only child is him right here." Jamal kissed JJ on top of his head, being dramatic as hell. Jamal gave me a paper from his pocket and I looked at it.

"What is this?" I opened it and read over the paternity test results.

"My proof." Jamal was sitting here looking at me like he just some shit.

"The fact that you had to go out and get tested lets me know there was a possibility. You lied to me and had sex with another broad, and I'm guessing unprotected. Do you know how bad I want to kill you every time I think about it?"

"Naomi, I fucked up. I'm sorry. Please just let me prove to you that I'll never do anything to hurt you again."

"Once my trust is lost, there's no getting it back. I forgave you once before but that was based on lies. I told you I'm done, and I meant that shit. I'm seeing somebody new anyway." The look of anger and hurt that flashed in Jamal's eyes made me smile.

"Fuck you mean, you seeing somebody? Seeing them do what?" Jamal seethed.

"He'll be doing a lot of shit when I allow him to." I smirked as I continued to taunt him.

"Let me get out of here before I end up choking the shit out of you," Jamal raged as he stood up. I stood with him just in case he tried to do something slick. My phone chimed, and it was a text from Monds. *Speak of the devil.*

Monds: How you doing beautiful? I was just thinking about you but didn't know if you was busy or not.

I smiled from ear to ear as I read his message. Next thing I know, me and my phone were slapped to the floor. My damn ears were ringing, and when I looked up at Jamal, I just smiled at him.

"You just gon' sit here in my face with the shit, bitch? You got me fucked up!" Jamal yelled as he paced back and forth.

I stood up, tasting the blood in my mouth and I saw red. Jamal looked at me and his face softened.

"Fuck, Na, I'm sor—" Stopping his sentence, I punched him in his mouth. I wasn't about to be the only one with a fucked-up lip. "A'ight, I deserved that, but keep your hands to yourself now."

"Fuck you," I said before charging him. I was throwing left and right hooks wherever they would land. Jamal struggled to dodge the hits, so he tried to wrestle me down.

"Stop! Damn!" Jamal screamed in my face when he finally got me down. This nigga was sitting on me and had my hands pinned over my head.

"Get the fuck off me," I spat. My chest heaved up and down and I was breathing like an angry bull. I had watched niggas beat Nicole's ass for whatever reason and I always said I would take a motherfuck-er's head off if they tried me like that.

"I'll move, but you got to let me leave. I'm sorry for putting my hands on you, but we're even." I looked at the damage I had done to him and I was proud. His mouth and nose were bleeding and I saw the small lump forming on his forehead.

Jamal let me up and JJ's cries distracted me from attacking again. Jamal took that opportunity to haul ass out the front door. He could get away now, but he'd have to see me for the next eighteen years. If I decided we were going to fight at every pick-up and drop off, then so be it. He had me fucked up.

"Ssshh, baby boy, it's okay." I bounced JJ in my arms until I got him calmed down. I knew he was fighting sleep, so I popped his paci-fier into his mouth, then went to lie him down in his crib. I learned from experience if I wanted JJ to go to sleep, then I had to just leave him by himself. I had his baby monitor and I could see every corner of the room, courtesy of his Auntie Wiz.

I heard my phone ringing, so I ran to get it. Seeing Monds Face-Timing me, I had to ignore it and sent him a text instead.

Me: Hey I'm trying to get my son to sleep, I'll call you later.
Monds: Okay beautiful I was just checking on you.

His message came seconds later, and even though my face was hurting, I smiled anyway. I went to the bathroom to assess the damage to my face and it wasn't as bad as I thought. Since my skin was so light, the bruise on my cheek was noticeable already. I already knew with a little concealer, I could hide it. For now, I was grabbing an ice pack and putting it on my face so it wouldn't swell.

The perfect idea popped into my head as I laid across the bed. Jamal was going to get his.

"HEY, BEAUTIFUL, THANKS FOR MEETING ME." Monds stood to greet me when I made it to the table.

"Thanks for making time for me. How's your day going so far?" It had been a few days since that incident with Jamal and I didn't really want to come out until my face healed.

"It's better now that I could see you. Is your son feeling better?"

"Huh?" That threw me for a loop, then I remembered I'd told him JJ wasn't feeling good. "Oh, he's better now, thanks for asking," I chuckled.

"Welcome to Gibsons. Can I start you two off with some drinks?" The waiter approached us, and I was already scanning the wine menu.

"I'll take some water with lemon, and a glass of Terlato, please," I said.

"Let's just make it a bottle of Terlato and add two glasses of water. We'll need a minute before we're ready to order, thank you." Monds was a grown man and everything about him had my body heating up.

"You should pay attention to the menu and not undressing me with your eyes." Monds gave me a panty-dropping smirk that made me clench my legs together.

"Don't flatter yourself, Cirmondo." I smiled from ear to ear and couldn't hide it if I tried. I hadn't felt this way since I'd met Jamal. I just hoped this wasn't a front, hiding who he really is.

When the server came back with our drinks, we were ready to order. Since I was trying to lose and keep my baby weight off me, I ordered a spicy lobster cobb salad while Monds ordered a skirt steak. It was only one o'clock, so I knew if he was going back to work, he was going to have the itis.

In the two months we'd been talking, Monds had taken me out just about every weekend, whether it was lunch or dinner. With our schedules, I didn't think it would work, but Monds was definitely showing me that he had potential. With me knocking on thirty, I was ready for something more solid. I wanted my next relationship to be my last, and that was why me and Monds agreed to take things slow and just date to get to know each other.

"Are you okay to drive?" Monds asked as he walked me to my car.

"Yeah, I'm good. Thanks for another wonderful date." I looked up at Monds and he bit his lip. I didn't know if it was the liquor or what, but I damn near jumped on this man, attacking him with my lips.

Monds' strong hands roamed my body until they landed on my ass. I moaned into his mouth and had to pull away before I did something I might regret.

"I'm sorry," he spoke and adjusted himself in his pants.

"It's okay, that was my fault. I'll see you later, though." I pecked his lips again, then got in the car. He closed my door and stood there until I pulled off. I didn't know what he was doing to me, but I was loving that shit.

I called Looney when I got to the stoplight and she answered on the first ring.

"Wassup, sissy?" I could hear the money counter in the background, so I already knew where she was.

"I'm about to pull up on you," I said before hanging up. I didn't want her asking any questions until I got there. I pulled up to the trap and Moe was just getting out her car.

Even better, I thought as I approached her.

"What you doing on this side of town?" Moe asked as I followed her to the back of the house.

"I'll tell you when we get down here, so I don't have to repeat myself." There were some armed men guarding the door, and they parted when they saw us.

The trap Looney ran looked like someone's grandma's house outside, but when you went inside, it had a different look. Upstairs was furnished like a home that was lived in, but downstairs, there were only tables lined up and a few chairs. I found Looney standing over some workers as they counted money.

"What's up, y'all?" Looney greeted us both with a hug. She stopped and looked at me like something was off. "What happened?"

"How long before you done here? I need y'all to roll with me somewhere."

"Do I need my gun wherever we're going?" Moe asked.

"You always need your gun," I replied.

"They counting the last of it now, give me like ten minutes." Me and Moe sat back and waited until Looney had everything locked up and we took my car.

"So, are you gon' tell me where we going, or do I gotta guess?"

"A'ight, Looney, Jamal had a hand problem the other day and it's time to teach him a lesson."

"Bitch, why you ain't call me when it happened? Are we killing him?" I looked over at Looney and she rubbed her hands together like Birdman.

"Because I handled it before, but I don't feel like I did enough. I tracked his phone over here on Paulina, so I know his guys over here, too."

"Say no more," Moe interrupted me. Looney looked back at her and they both had devious smiles on their faces. We pulled up to where Jamal's phone was, and I parked a few cars behind his car.

"If we go in the house, that's a setup, so I'm gon' make his alarm go off and we rush him when he come out. Got it?"

"Yup," they chanted.

"Good, come on." I hopped out and kicked Jamal's tires. His alarm started blaring, but he shut it off without coming out, so I did it again.

"What the fuck?" I heard his voice when he got closer to us.

"What's good, Mal?" Looney and Moe stepped out first, and I heard Jamal chuckle.

"What's good, Looney, what you doing out here?"

"What you think she doing out here?" Jamal turned quickly when he heard my voice behind him. Before he could get a word out, I punched him in the mouth, kicking off the plan. He was getting hit from everywhere and chose to ball up on the ground instead of fighting back.

Once they started stomping him with those Timbs on, I stopped them. "Let's go, that's enough. Nina, let's go!" We hopped in my car and I sped off. I had to drive past where Jamal was, and we saw him trying to help himself up.

"Biihhh!" We all busted out laughing at his expense.

"That shit was funny as hell. You think he gon' tell somebody we beat his ass like that?" Moe asked us.

"Hell nah, he won't be able to come to the hood no mo'." We laughed all the way back to the trap where I dropped them off at. My phone vibrated in the cupholder and Jamal's name popped up.

Baby daddy: Are we even now?

I smirked before responding.

Me: I don't know yet, I guess we gotta wait and see.

13

ECHO "EJ"

"AAAHH! Please stop, I swear I don't know anything!"

"You fuckin' lying!" Moe yelled and sent another blow to this guy's ribs.

This was the original driver of my missing truck. Paul had been with me for a couple years and I had never had a problem until now. This nigga wanted to say he had food poison and had somebody cover for him. The fuck this nigga thought he worked at, Target or some shit? Switching shifts and shit.

"Where's my truck, Paul?" I asked again as I filed my nails. I had waited long enough while I was in the hospital before we made some moves to find out who had a death wish.

"EJ, you know my loyalty with you. I don't know what happened to the truck. I didn't even know shit went missing until y'all rolled up on me. I swear on my life."

"Would you swear on your wife's life?" I asked as Paul's wife was drug into the warehouse, kicking and screaming.

"Wh-what is this? Please, just let her go, she don't know anything," Paul pleaded.

"I believe she doesn't know anything, but you do. Until you

decide to give me what I want, I'm going to see if I can get it out of her. Strap her to the table," I directed the foot soldiers, who had Paul's wife. Once they had her down, I walked to her and she looked terrified.

"See, I didn't want to bring you in this, but unfortunately for you, your husband is a liar and a thief," I explained as I brought out a bucket of water. I had someone holding a towel on her face while I poured water over her. I didn't know who was screaming louder between her and Paul.

"I'll tell you what you want, but please just stop. I'll help you." Paul was crying like a bitch as he watched his wife lie still on the table. She wasn't dead, yet, just a little fucked up from drowning.

"Speak, and quick, before I change my mind."

"That nigga Wayne hit me up and said he'd pay me fifteen thousand to play sick. I didn't know what he had up his sleeve, but we needed that money." Paul's head dropped as he let out more silent tears.

"You should've called me the second he approached you. I can't trust you, Paul, and I can't have someone walking freely if I can't trust him."

Pew! Pew!

Before he could lift his head to look at me, I sent two bullets into his head. "Bury them together and clean this place out," I instructed. I needed to get home before Malik or the babies woke up. I knew they were going to be getting up for a feeding soon, so I was on a time limit. When I got the call that my people had snatched up this driver, I couldn't sleep if I didn't come out and handle this myself.

I stripped out of my bloody clothes and left them to get burned with everything else. I made it back to Malik's house and pulled into the garage. Even though I hadn't found my product or truck yet, I still felt a little closer to getting it.

"YOU SNEAKING out the house like you going to meet a nigga."

Malik was sitting in the dark, but flicked the lights on when I walked in.

"Shit, Malik, don't do shit like that." I put my gun down on the counter.

"Where were you?"

"Out. What you doing up?"

"Echo, don't do that shit! We supposed to be moving together in this shit. I don't need you sneaking out the house to do some shit behind my back. You don't trust me or something?"

"Listen, baby, it wasn't nothing personal. I got a call that my presence was needed, and I didn't have time to wake you up."

"That's bullshit."

"No, it's not. The same way you want to protect me, I did the same for you. At the end of the day, you're a detective, Malik. There's some shit that I do that I don't want you in the middle of. If anything was ever to happen, I don't want you caught in the worse of it."

"Let me decide what's too much for me and what's not. A'ight?"

"Okaaaay, baby, I'm sorry. Don't be mad at me." I poked my bottom lip out and I could tell Malik was falling right into my trap.

"I don't know what to do with your ass, man." Malik smirked at me, and I had to cross my legs to stop the juices from running onto the floor. "Come here."

As I took a step towards him, I heard cries coming from the baby monitor. "That little girl is a cock blocker already," I laughed. Even though I wasn't cleared for anything, I could still suck some dick or something. I felt like it had been years since I'd had some action.

"Leave my baby alone. Come on, li'l nasty-ass girl, and put that gun up." I followed Malik upstairs and locked my gun in the safe before going to the nursery. Malik changed Eva's diaper and fed her the bottle I had pumped earlier, while I changed and fed Elijah.

It took a little minute to get the twins on the same schedule since Elijah came home a week after Eva did. If it wasn't for Malik's mama coming over every day when Malik left, I think I would've been lost my mind. I could tell Eva is the one who was going to give us a run for our money. It was like she screamed just to see how loud she could get. Elijah never made a peep unless I was taking too long to feed him. For these two to be twins, they were complete opposites.

∞

THE NEXT MORNING

When I opened my eyes this morning, I had to lay here for a few extra seconds. Malik was moving around the room, getting dressed, and I watched him.

"Malani's coming over today instead of Ma. I'll call you when I get a free minute. Love you, baby." Malik gave me a kiss before rushing out.

I grabbed the baby monitor from Malik's nightstand and had to thank the man upstairs that the twins were still asleep. I went to empty my bladder and brush my teeth while I had the time. I took a quick shower, making sure to hit everything twice before getting out. Since I didn't plan on leaving the house, I slipped on a tank and some sweatpants before going downstairs. I quickly learned that if it was something I wanted to get done for myself, I had to do it while the twins were asleep.

The doorbell chimed while I was eating, and I saw Malani from the cameras I had Wiz install. This was the only way I agreed to stay here. I had to feel that me and my babies were secure at all times.

"Good morning, sunshine. You're looking good, Echo. I need whatever workout you been doing. It don't even look like you just gave birth to twins." Malani came in the house, full of energy as always.

"I haven't been able to work out how I want, just watching what I eat for now." My big bump was gone, but I still had a little beer belly.

The second I got the okay from my doctor, I was going back to hitting the gym hard.

"I love to eat too much for that. You probably be eating that damn rabbit food. No thank you," Malani said with her nose in the air.

"Your ass don't need to lose weight anyway. What's been going on, though? How's school and shit?" I asked, sitting down at the island where my food was.

"It's going good. I made the Dean's list again."

"Congratulations, Lani, I'm proud of you, for real."

"Thanks, Echo. I had to work my ass off just to prove to my dad I wasn't wasting his money in college. I've been working on something I want to show you, too." Malani went to her bag and handed me the sketchbook I'd bought for her.

"Damn, this shit go hard, G." I flipped the pages in her book and was impressed with the drawings she had. She was a beast when it came to portraits especially. When I got to the portrait she'd started of the twins, it made me tear up a little bit.

"I know it's not perfect, but I still got some work to do before it's finished."

"Besides some shading, this is great."

"So do you plan on opening *The Gallery* back up?" Malani brought up the subject I had been trying to avoid for the longest.

"Honestly, I don't know. I was thinking about selling the place." I shrugged my shoulders.

"What? Why the hell would you do that?" I paused to think of an answer. I didn't really want to tell her I had to figure out who was trying to ruin my empire before I got back to my art gallery.

"Well, ever since I got arrested in there, the vibe has been off. I can't really bring myself to open the doors back up," I half-lied.

"If I was you, I would tell Leaky to buy me another building. It's his damn fault all this happened anyway." Malani had a stank look on her face that had me laughing.

"It's not his fault, he was doing his job. It's the person's fault who sent him to my establishment in the first place." I smiled, thinking of the dirt nap Bud and Play were taking right now.

"Seriously, Echo, you were doing so many great things for the community. Are you really just going to give up on all of that right now? I still got so much to learn from you."

"Okaaaay, girl, damn. You irky." I playfully rolled my eyes at her.

"I love you, too," Malani giggled.

Eva started wailing, signaling it was time to get up and get on baby duty. Malani had really given me a lot to think about. *The Gallery* wasn't just a place for me to sell my art, it was my sanctuary. I was serious when I told her the vibe was off when I went there. I tried to burn sage and everything to try to get rid of that negative energy, but nothing worked. I doubt I would find another location as perfect as that one, but I was going to try.

14

NINA "LOONEY"

"OOOHH, SHIT," I moaned as I threw my head back. I was supposed to be on my way to meet up with Moe and Wiz, but Spade just wanted to eat my kitty so bad. My dumb ass gave in and somehow I ended up butter ball naked, riding his dick.

"Damn, Neen, I don't wanna pull out." Spade had a death grip on my hips and I was going to break his damn nose if he tried to nut in me.

"You better let me the fuck go, Daniel," I warned, biting hard on my bottom lip. I was on the verge of my own release.

"Shut the fuck up." Spade flipped us over so he was on top now. "Put that ass up."

Slap!

The slap he landed on my ass had me creaming before he even put it back in. "Freaky ass." I could hear the smile in Spade's voice even if I couldn't see him. He started off with deep, slow strokes, hitting my spot every time, thanks to his curve. He went from slow strokes to beating it up with no remorse. Had my ass screaming to the heavens and anybody else within a five mile radius.

Spade pulled out quickly, making me turn around. "Gggrrr, shit!"

Spade growled as he caught his nut in his hand. "Yo' phone over there lighting up, but I wasn't gon' stop to tell you that while I was knee deep in them guts."

"Damn, Spade, move." I pushed him out the way and got out the bed. I saw I was already running behind schedule and I needed to shower again.

"Keep fuckin' playing with them, I almost dropped this shit on the bed." I ignored his ass as I made my way to the shower. I already knew Moe was going to have some shit to talk and I didn't have time for all that.

"I'm out. I'll be by to pick the money up from yo' trap when I'm done with this meeting, so you better make sure them niggas ain't been slacking. EJ been itching to put a hole in some mothafuckas' heads since that truck got stole. Don't let that person be you. Love you."

It took me another thirty minutes to get across town with the fucked-up traffic. It was the middle of November and everybody forgot how to drive when snow started falling.

"Took yo' ass long enough," Moe complained when I walked into the distribution warehouse. "I hope you was at least working."

"Mind the business that pays you, G. I'm here right now, so what's up? How them numbers looking?" I directed my attention to Wiz, who was tapping away on her laptop.

"Shit looking good, even better than before. We made more than enough profit to double the shipment we lost."

"*WE* didn't lose a damn thing. That dead nigga Paul lost it," I reminded her.

"Same shit, man. We all are responsible for the shit that happens in this organization."

"Save the lecture and shit, man." I rolled my eyes to the ceiling.

"Do you have any leads on where the truck is now? I know they had to stop just once," Moe asked Wiz.

"The last I saw, it stopped in the middle of nowhere. That tells me they either ditched the truck or found the tracking device and got rid of it."

"We need more than that to bring back to Echo, man." I shook my head. "Is that it?"

"Nah. I've been noticing the alarm at *The Gallery*. When I pulled up the tapes, it's the same woman popping up every day. I don't know who she is or what she wants, but she shows up around two in the afternoon every day." I checked my watch and saw it was a quarter past one.

"A'ight, don't put EJ up on game yet, let us go check it out. Hit one of us when you find something out."

"Be careful, Looney," Wiz called out to my back. Ever since I'd gotten shot, they'd been trying to treat me like I was fragile or some shit. I was born for this shit and wasn't no little-ass bullet going to stop me.

"You think whoever this is is connected to the truck being stolen?" Moe asked as she drove to *The Gallery*.

"I don't know, but we about to find out. It's probably one of them nosy-ass reporters looking for a story or something." I sat back in my seat and enjoyed the ride. The roads were slick, so I knew it was going to take us longer than usual.

"Look at this shit." Moe pointed when she parked in back of EJ's building. A woman was standing at the back door, looking like she was trying to break in.

"Aye!" We hopped out with our guns and rushed to the door. "Fuck is you doing here?"

The woman turned around and there was something familiar about her. She was an older woman, probably early fifties. "I-I was looking for the owner. Is she around?" she stuttered.

"We asking the questions here, and I'm only going to ask one more time. What the fuck is you doing here?" I had my gun pointed to her forehead, and so did Moe. It was too damn cold to be out here playing with this bitch.

"EJ is my daughter and she's in danger. I'm trying to save

her life."

Bam!

Moe cracked her ass over the head and she hit the snow hard. "Damn, bitch, you could've just told her to get in the trunk. Now we gotta carry her ass."

"I'm ready to get back in some heat and she was playing. Come on." Moe grabbed her up by the collar and I got her feet. Once we tossed her in the trunk, we headed to the warehouse.

Me: Surprise party.

I sent the text to the rest of the girls and prepared for the craziness that was bound to happen. When it came to big decisions, we made sure to include each other, no matter what. With this broad claiming to be Echo's mother, I think she needed to be here more than anybody else. DB showed up shortly after we did since she was closer, then Naomi. They both looked at the woman confused.

"Who is this?" Naomi asked us.

"I hope I'm not wasting my time. It's too cold to be playing with y'all today." EJ walked through the door and stopped when she saw who we had tied to a chair. It was like she was frozen in place; she didn't move or say anything.

"Echo?"

"What is she doing here?! Huh? Bitch, what you doing here?!" Echo snapped and jumped on the woman so fast, beating the shit out of her. She was still out from Moe knocking her over the head, but the combos EJ gave to her sure enough woke her up.

"Echo, calm down. Who is this?" It took all of us to pull her off this woman.

"Kill her. I don't care what happens," Echo said, then stormed out.

"What the hell was that?" DB asked the question I was sure we were all thinking.

"I don't know, but we need to figure out what she's here for. Just keep Echo out of it right now." Naomi gave direction, then left me and Moe to get to work.

15

ECHO "EJ"

"The past will often attack the present with the pain of your memories." -Seiichi Kirima

MY BLOOD WAS BOILING as I whipped in and out of traffic. I didn't care about the other people on the road or traffic laws. I had to get far away from that warehouse before I lost my shit even more.

"Hey, Echo, did you have an appointment?" Dr. Fidel's assistant greeted me as I marched inside. "You can't go back there!"

"Fidel, I need you. You get the fuck out." I pointed to the patient she was with.

"Echo, you can't just barge in here. I still have half of a session here. Give me a minute." Dr. Fidel stood to try to show me out, but I wouldn't budge.

"I need you now," I said sternly.

"Mark, we can reschedule your appointment and you won't be charged for this."

"Hell naw, she gotta wait until I'm done," Mark argued.

Click.

"This is me asking nicely. Get your shit and get out." Me having my gun to his head was all the motivation he needed as he ran out the door.

"Was that really necessary? Have a seat, you know the routine. And I'm going to need that gun in the basket, too."

I did what she said and laid across the chaise. I had to get my thoughts in order because they were all over the place. The good thing is Dr. Fidel waited patiently without interrupting me.

"She came back," I finally said.

"Who came back?"

"My mo—Elaine, the woman who birthed and ditched me."

"I'm guessing it wasn't a cheerful reunion. Did you give her a chance to explain why she was here, or why she left?" I chuckled. "Okay, I'll take that as a no. How did you feel when you saw her?"

"I was pissed, and I snapped. If it wasn't for my sisters pulling me off her... I don't know, man."

"What about seeing her made you so pissed?"

"Why come back now? After years. I used to cry and pray that she'd come back to save me from the shit I went through and she didn't! Now more than twenty years later, she pops up, talking about she's trying to save me. I should've killed her myself," I ranted.

"Okay, I didn't hear that. I understand the pain and resentment you feel towards your mother—"

"She's not my mother," I interrupted her.

"Elaine. But we've worked so hard to get you where you are now, let's not backslide. Think about forgiveness, or at least listening to what she has to say. If you want, you can do it here."

"Nah, Doc, that won't happen."

"The weak can never forgive. Forgiveness is the attributes of the strong. Ghandi said that and I believe it. There's nothing weak about you, Echo, and you know it. You don't have to make any decisions now, just think on it."

"Okay, I'll do that." I heard my phone vibrating nonstop, so I guessed it was time for me to go. "I'll make sure you're compensated for today, sorry about that."

"Anytime, just maybe call first," Dr. Fidel said laughing.

I grabbed my phones and gun before leaving. I saw some missed calls from Malani and Malik, so I called her back first.

"Hey, I just left the house. Malik is there now, and the babies were sleep."

"Okay, thank you, Lani. Sorry about running out like that. We can set something up for us to get together another time and talk art," I offered.

"It's fine. And I'd love that, just let me know when."

"All right, I'll talk to you later." I hung up and continued my drive home. Malik was peeking through the blind when I pulled in the driveway, and I just hoped he wasn't about to start any shit.

"Everything okay?" Malik asked as I walked through the door.

"Yeah. Are the twins still sleep?"

"Where were you? I came in thinking something happened to you, then you're not answering the phone—" I stopped Malik's questioning by pressing my lips into his. I didn't want to hear anything right now.

"I'm not ready to talk about it, but I'll let you know. Don't look at me like that, it's not like that. It's personal."

"Okay, baby girl. What's for dinner?" I was shocked that he'd just dropped the subject like that.

"What do you have a taste for?"

"You, honestly, but since I can't have that, I'll settle for some lasagna."

I went to the kitchen and took out what I was going to need to make the lasagna. My mind went back to Elaine and her telling Looney and Moe she was trying to save my life. Grabbing my phone, I sent a text to the group chat.

Me: I know you didn't clean up after the party. Leave it for me.
Na: Are you sure?
Me: Yeah I'm sure.

DB: *Okay.*
Looney: *Got you, boss lady.*
Moe: *Heard.*
Na: *Call me!*

I already knew Naomi was going to try to be a peace maker, but I didn't need that right now. I was going to handle Elaine my own way, on my own time.

∞

IT HAD BEEN a few days since Elaine had popped up and I still had her tied up in the warehouse. Lucky for her, she was being fed and given water three times a day. I planned to go back there today and see what she wanted, but I wanted her to sweat a little more. I'd been watching the cameras in the warehouse, trying to see if I could read her. She seemed too calm for a person being held against their will, so I needed to see what she was really doing here.

"I'm going in here by myself, y'all just wait out here," I said to Naomi and the girls.

"Finally, Echo. Are you finally coming to hear what I have to say?" Elaine asked when I walked into the warehouse.

"You got three minutes to convince me to let you live. Go." I hit the timer on my phone and stared at her. Elaine stared back at me in shock. "Two minutes and thirty seconds," I reminded her.

"I know where your truck is," Elaine blurted.

"What truck?"

"Come on, Echo, I know what you really do and it's not that art. You do have a real talent, though. I even have a piece in my—"

"Shut the fuck up!" I yelled, kicking her chair over. "Tell me where my shit is." I pressed my gun into her mouth and cocked it.

"Okay, okay, wait," she said, muffled. "It's Rick, your stepfather."

That name sounded familiar, but I couldn't put a face to the name yet.

"Why does Rick have my truck, and how did you know about it?"

"He's been watching you for a while, since that trial. That's how I knew where your art gallery was. He's had people following you for months, trying to track your moves and couldn't. Somehow, he got in contact with your driver and paid him to bring your product to him. I can take you to where he's keeping it."

"You was going to do that anyway, and I will peel your face off if you try any funny shit," I warned.

"I won't, I promise. I just wanted to see you, Echo. I never wanted to harm you in any way, but I think Rick is, that's why I came. I heard him mentioning your babies and knew I had to come find you." Something in me snapped when she mentioned my babies and I lost it. I went across her face with the butt of my gun and continued to hit her until I was being dragged off her.

"Echo, chill!" Naomi shouted in my ear.

"Bitch, let that be the last time my kids are on your mind." I struggled to get out the bear hug Naomi had me in. "Let me go, I'm good!" This heifer didn't listen and continued to pull me out the door.

"What the fuck, Echo? Is that what you call cool, calm, and collected?"

"Fuck that shit! This bitch bringing up my babies, talking about somebody threatened them, it's war!"

"And you know we're going to be there next to you through it all, but you gotta use your head. You always preaching to us about calculated moves and moving in the shadows. You can't be out here acting like you in a western movie, shooting shit."

The doors to the warehouse opened and Looney and Moe walked out. Looney was laughing, and Moe just shook her head.

"What?" I asked them.

"Nothing at all. I don't want no smoke," Looney joked. "She still breathing, just gon' be fucked up for a little bit."

"That's too bad. Call the doctor and make sure this bitch don't

die. I need to know everything about this nigga Rick and his operation before we make our moves. In the meantime, I want everybody
to move shit around again. She claim this nigga's been watching us for
a while. I'm not taking no more L's from anybody. I'm getting extra
security on every house and on you all during drop-off and
pick-up days.

"Moe, I want you to be the one to come back in a few days and
get what you can out of her. Everybody else, just be alert and go back
to business as usual. I got to go."

I walked away from them and hopped in my waiting car. I guess
it was time for me to update Malik on what was going on.

16

MALIK "DETECTIVE STEVENS"

"STEVENS!" Sergeant Gills called me the second I walked to my office door from lunch. His face was balled up and I had to stop and think if I had done something.

"What's going on, Serge?" I asked as I approached him.

"I need to speak with you in private. Come on." Instead of going to his office, we went towards the conference room and I was confused, for real. I started to panic, thinking maybe he had found something out about me and Echo.

"Congratulations!" I was shocked to see my colleagues standing around with a bunch of balloons and gifts.

"What's all this about?" I asked, laughing and shaking hands.

"We heard about your new bundles of joys that you've neglected to tell us about. Consider this your baby shower," Sergeant Gill informed me.

"Aaww, man, y'all ain't have to do this." They really had it decorated in here with the whole nine, even had a cake. After showing some pictures of Eva and Elijah, we started getting calls, so we had to split up.

"Stevens, you're blessed. I don't know why you chose to keep all of this a secret. Who's the unlucky lady that's stuck with you for the next eighteen years?" Sergeant Gill joked.

"Ha-ha, very funny. But it's someone I've been dealing with for a while now. I was actually thinking about making an honest woman out of her."

Sergeant Gill whistled. "Marriage? That's a big step, man. You can't just go around giving anybody your last name just because she popped some babies out for you."

"Thanks for the advice, but I love her." I smiled, thinking about Echo.

"Well, I can definitely see you're smitten. Well, I hope to meet her soon as well as those precious babies. Congratulations again." He walked away, leaving me to my thoughts.

I hated that I couldn't really be open about our relationship because of the investigation I led against her. The last thing I wanted was to lose everything I had worked for because I fell in love. I grabbed the gifts from the conference room and loaded my trunk up with everything. My personal phone beeped when I got back behind my desk and Echo's name flashed across the screen.

"What's going on, baby? Everything okay?" I asked.

"Yeah, I was just calling to see if you can pick the twins up from my ma's house. I'm handling some business and I don't know when I'll be done. If you can't do it, it's okay."

"I got you, baby girl, relax. You talking like those aren't my babies, too. It's cool. You don't need my help with anything, right?" I didn't know what business she was handling, but I wanted her to be safe.

"Nah, baby, I don't need assistance with this. I shouldn't be late."

"Okay, be safe, love you."

"Love you too," Echo cooed before hanging up.

I looked over a few cases I knew involved the Coke Gurls organization and got rid of as much evidence as I could without it looking suspicious. These were cases I knew would never be solved. I just wanted to make sure that if they were assigned to someone else, they wouldn't connect Echo or anyone close to her. Once that was done, I packed up to leave for the day.

"Hey there, Malik, come on in," Ms. Sharp greeted me with a smile. I stepped in and it smelled like she was cooking.

"How are you doing, Ms. Sharp? I hope the babies weren't too much for you today." I hugged her, then kicked the door closed.

"I keep telling you to call me Mama Lani. You're a part of this family now. And my sweet grandbabies would never be too much for me." She smiled brightly. She started walking towards the back of the house and I stopped her.

"I actually wanted to talk to you before we get them." I was a little nervous, and I think Mama Lani could tell by my face.

"Sure, sweetie. Come on to the kitchen, so I can check my roast." It was only a quarter past four and she was already cooking dinner. I wasn't surprised because my mother was the same way.

"Well, you know I love Echo more than anything, probably even more since she had the babies. I don't know how much Echo spoke to you about our situation, but we been through a lot."

"Oh, you mean you arresting my baby? I know all about that," she called me out. I dropped my head in shame. "You were doing your job. Echo don't hold it against you, and I don't either... anymore," she chuckled.

"I was just following my oath and if I could take it back, I would. But, I wanted to talk to you to see how you'd feel if I asked Echo to marry me." I finally looked up at Mama Lani and she was smiling so big, it was spread across her face.

"You know I would love that. I can definitely see a difference in my baby and I feel like I can thank you for that. You have my blessing." I let out a breath I didn't know I was holding when she said that.

"Thank you, now maybe I can get you to come ring shopping with me?"

"Just let me know when and I'll be ready." Eva's crying in the baby monitor broke up the moment we were having, so I went to get her. Even though the twins are fraternal, they were both a perfect mixture of me and Echo. Eva looked more like Echo with her mocha-colored skin, and when she pouts, I saw Echo's whole face. Elijah was my complexion, but he looked to have half my face and half Echo's. Whenever I looked at the family I was building, I felt like the luckiest man in America.

Mama Lani helped me bundle them up in their car seats. I went out to warm the car up and noticed a black sedan parked across the street. I wouldn't have thought anything of it, but that same one was sitting there when I pulled up. I could clearly see figures inside and I got a feeling that something wasn't right.

I took my gun from the holster and walked towards the car. Whoever was in it peeled off down the street, but not before I got the license plate number.

Me: Can you check these plates for me, asap. IL plates ZP 77821

I sent the text to Wiz and she replied right away.

Wiz: Got it. Give me five.

Wiz and Naomi seemed to be the only ones who welcomed me with open arms. I guess the other ones were still on defense about me being the law and all.

"Hey, Mama Lani, did you want to come stay with us for a while? I know it'll help us a lot." I wasn't comfortable leaving her here when there was a strange car sitting outside her house.

"I know what you're trying to do, and you can forget it. Echo made sure this place could be locked down like Fort Knox. I'm not a rookie when it comes to protecting myself and my home, I'm fine."

"Okay, well, don't hesitate to call if something doesn't feel right." I grabbed the car seats and the plates of food Mama Lani made me take.

I took the long way home, then circled the block in case I was being followed. I pulled into the garage and saw Echo's car still parked. I knew she had started using her driver again, so I wasn't sure if she was here or not.

"What are you in here making all that noise for, little mama?" I picked Eva up and instantly, she stopped crying. This little girl knew she had everybody wrapped around her finger. All she had to do was make a little peep and somebody would pick her up.

"I heard her little lungs sounding off from outside." Echo came through the door and took her coat off. She was dressed in a pants suit, looking like she had just left from court.

"You already know how she is when she not getting attention. Sort of like her mama," I joked.

"Yeah, whatever. So, where did you see the car that you texted Wiz about?" Echo walked to where we were in the living room and took Elijah from me.

"Damn, she called you and didn't bother hitting me up. The car was parked outside your mom's house, and they sped off when I tried to approach them. Who was it?"

"It was a stolen car so I'm not sure. I do have to talk to you about some stuff, though. Let's get them settled first." We both took a baby, fed, bathed and laid them down in their nursery. Since Mama Lani had sent some food home with me, we didn't have to worry about dinner. I warmed the food while Echo sat at the dining table.

After a moment of silence, Echo finally started talking. "So, my mama showed up last week," Echo said, putting a forkful of food into her mouth. "My biological mother."

"Woah, and what happened?"

"Before or after I tried to beat her half to death?" Echo laughed like what she had said was a joke, but I knew better than that.

"What the fuck? Why?"

"I had a truck come up missing a while back and, come to find out, it was her bitch-ass husband who took it. I don't know why. She said something about him watching our every move, and when she mentioned Eva and Eli, I snapped."

"So what's the plan?" I asked, ready for whatever.

"He wants a war, so I'm gon' give it to him. I already got extra security around, but I want to dead the issue before any real threat comes our way. I'm not asking you to get in the middle of this—"

"Whenever you move, I'll be ready. I told you I'm with you

through whatever. But after this, then what? How long are we going to have to worry about somebody gunning for your head? It's not just about you anymore, Echo."

"I know that, and I plan to retire and go legit after all threats are ceased. The girls don't know it yet and they'll be pissed. Well, Looney and Moe will be."

"Why?"

"Because it's all or nothing. If I step down, then they'll be forced to do the same. After ten years of watching over my back, I'm ready to live a normal life with my babies."

"Damn, what about me?" I feigned hurt.

"You're not going anywhere, you're stuck." We both laughed and continued to eat. I was glad she said that because I didn't plan on leaving her. This is forever.

17

NADIA "WIZ"

"WELCOME TO MYXED. OH, HEY, NADIA," the receptionist of DB's salon greeted me when I walked in.

"Hey, is DB free?"

"Yeah, she's waiting on you." I thanked her and went to the back where DB's station was.

Knock. Knock.

"Come in! Hey, babe, I figured it was you." DB embraced me, then went back to organizing her station.

"Yeah, I'm long overdue for some TLC in this head. I was thinking about adding some color or something." I stood in the mirror and ran my fingers through my hair. I caught DB smirking at me in the mirror. "What?" I asked her.

"Bitch, you getting some dick. Who is he?"

"What? I'm just trying to switch it up." I was trying to avoid DB's eyes because I knew she could read my lies.

"Spill it or I'm not doing nothing." She sat down and folded her arms across her chest.

"Ohhhh my God, okay. But don't say nothing because I don't even know if it'll go anywhere."

"Who I'ma tell? Girl, who is it, shit?"

"Jay," I whispered.

"Excuse me, who?" DB put her hand to her ear and leaned closer to me.

"Jay, hoe!" I playfully pushed her.

"Jay? Moe's crazy-ass brother? How in the world did that happen? Come on." She waved me over to the shampoo bowl.

"I don't know, it just sort of happened. I had to go on a run with him to test out the new routes and I saw a different side of him. He's usually wild and irritating, but those few days we spent together, he was sweet. And before you ask, no, I didn't give him any nookie. But we are going out tonight, that's why I want everything to be right."

"Say no more, you know I got you." DB caped me then got to work.

"So what's been new with you?"

"Nothing exciting like you, but I have been thinking about expanding. I get a lot of inquiries from people in Atlanta and Miami, so that might be my next move."

"Yessss, baby, I'm so proud of you. I think you should go for it." I was genuinely excited for my friend.

"I don't know, I can't really leave right now. It's too much going on to just leave you all hanging."

"Darbie, trust me when I say that none of us would fault you for going to secure that bag. We'll miss you like hell, but you know we got your back through whatever."

"After all this is handled, then I might see how it's looking for me," DB said. Two hours later, I was finally headed home. I saw a car parked in my driveway and rolled my eyes when Nicole stepped out.

"What do you want now, Nicole? I'm not giving you no more money," I let her know when I got out my car.

"I'm not here for that. I really just wanted to talk to you."

Reluctantly, I let her in and took a seat to hear what she wanted. "I have somewhere to be, so I don't have all day."

"Are you going on a date? I love your hair like that," she complimented me. Darbie had my hair bone straight and had added some highlights in it.

"I'm sure that's not what you came here for," I said dryly and crossed my arms across my chest.

"Right, sorry. Well, I've been doing good in the program you got me in and I wanted to thank you."

"You're welcome."

"And I wanted to see if maybe you can talk to your sisters about getting together. And maybe see about Naomi letting me meet my grandson." Nicole snuck that last part in.

"No, I'm not getting in the middle of that shit. I'll put the bug in their ear about you wanting to sit down and make amends, but that's it."

"Please, Nadia. Christmas is coming, and I just want to be there with my grandson. Let me make up for being such a terrible mother to y'all." Nicole started sniffling and I knew it was a part of her plot to try to sucker me into doing what she wanted.

"All I can do is mention it to Na, I'm not advocating for you."

"Thank you, Nadia. I promise I'm better and I'll prove it."

"Okay, I have to get ready, soooo..." I let my sentence trail off.

"I get it, it's time for me to go. You know you can call me sometimes. I hate that I have to pop up on you just to see you."

"All right, Nicole, have a good night, and make sure you're back for curfew," I called out as she walked out the door. I might've acted tough with Nicole, but I still checked on her through the program director. Not only because I had spent hella money to get her in, but at the end of the day, she was our mother and I wanted to see her doing well.

I watched Nicole pull out of my driveway before I went to find the perfect outfit for tonight. I didn't know where we were going, but Jay had told me to dress comfortable. Since it was cold out, I picked acid wash blue jeans and a long sleeve bodysuit with a deep V-cut. I was going to try my luck and wear some heels and hope I didn't bust my ass trying to be cute. Jay told me to be ready at eight and it was four o'clock right now. That gave me plenty of time to do some work before it was time to get ready.

Since we had found out that we were being watched, I had to move everything around, from changing security codes to moving around the money we had in overseas accounts. Echo didn't know how much this Rick nigga knew about our operation, or how far he was willing to go, so this was just extra precaution. While it was fresh on my mind, I decided to text Naomi.

Me: Na I'm about to ask you something and I want you to keep an open mind.

Instantly, I saw the three dots pop up, indicating that she was responding.

Naomi: What?

Me: Nicole has been stopping by and she wants to make amends and be a part of JJ's life.

Naomi: Negative.

Me: Come on Na, she's still our mother, and she's clean. I made sure of it.

Naomi: I don't know, I have to think about it.

Me: That's all I ask. Now can you see if Looney would be down for a sit down too? Thanks, love you!

I sent the text and put Naomi on do not disturb because I know she was going to curse me out.

18

NAOMI "NA"

"Sometimes the bad things that happen in our lives put us directly on the path to the best things that will ever happen to us."

"THIS HEFFA THINK SHE SLICK," I said aloud to myself. Wiz knew Looney was not going to take that news well, and I had to deal with her attitude.

"Everything okay?" Monds asked as he rubbed my feet.

"Yeah, it's just my sister trying to plan a family reunion." I chuckled and shook my head.

"I'm guessing you're not here for it?"

"It's not that, but my mother wasn't really the best growing up, so our relationship is pretty much nonexistent." Me and Monds were building something and I kind of trusted him, I had just never shared the back story of Nicole. It was always out of sight out of mind with Nicole.

"I can tell that's a sensitive subject, so I won't push it. So, what's your plans for the holidays?"

"I don't know yet. I might just do something small with my sisters. Since it's the first holiday where we have children, we might do it big."

"Well, if you want, you're invited to the dinner my family has every Christmas Eve. I might've mentioned you and they want to meet you."

"Oh, um... okay." I'm not going to lie and say I wasn't nervous because I was. With Jamal, all he had was his siblings like me, so I didn't have to go through that whole meeting the family thing.

"If it's too much right now, I understand—" I stopped Monds' rambling when I straddled him and mashed our lips together.

"I'll be there," I spoke against his lips. Monds took control of our kiss and stuck his tongue into my mouth, which I happily took.

"Mmm," I moaned into his mouth, his strong hands gripped my eyes. I felt him growing under me and decided to take it further. I pulled my shirt over my head and my breasts were sitting right in his face. I was happy I hadn't worn a bra.

"You sure you want to do this?" Monds asked, looking me in the eyes. I nodded 'yes' and Monds wasted no time attacking my breasts.

"Wait." I stopped him because my breasts were starting to hurt. I was embarrassed to see milk leaking out.

"Oh shit, my bad," Monds laughed, and I felt my face turn red. "Li'l man just gon' have to share today," he joked and went back to his assault. He laid me on the couch and slid my pants down.

"Oohh shit, baby," I moaned when I felt Monds' stiff tongue across my clit. My back was arched, and I damn near raised all the way off the couch. His head game was driving me crazy and I was on the edge of cumming.

"Let it go, Na baby," Monds spoke against my kitty. The vibration from his deep voice sent me over the edge and I came so hard, I was seeing stars. Monds licked up every drop and didn't stop.

"Aaahh, wait. Stop," I said breathlessly, pushing his head away. I watched through hooded eyes as Monds undressed and took a condom out his wallet. His dick was a nice size, probably nine inches, and it was nice and thick, just how I liked it.

"Let me do that." I stopped him from opening the condom. I licked around the head of his dick, tasting the pre cum that oozed out. You could always tell if a man took care of himself by the taste of his nut.

"Shiiiitt," Monds cursed when I deep throated his monster. His hands went from my head, to his side, until he finally locked them behind his head. "Fuck, Na, do that shit," he encouraged me. I made sure to get extra sloppy for him and had slobber dripping down my chin. I relaxed my throat so I could take him all the way back, and played with his balls. That was something I had learned could snatch the soul right out of a nigga, and that was exactly what happened.

"Fuuucckkk," Monds grunted as he came in my mouth. I swallowed it and smirked because I owned his soul now, and he knew it. I sucked and jerked him back to life and rolled the condom on with my mouth.

I saw another side of Monds when he snatched me up off the floor and picked me up. He slammed me on his dick and fucked the shit out of me. I was enjoying the feeling of our bodies connecting; I wasn't worried about him dropping me.

An hour later, we were laid out on the living room floor, breathing like we had just ran a marathon.

"Damn, Na," Monds finally spoke.

"I know, right. It was definitely worth the wait. Now, let's go to the shower so I can show you what else I can do." Usually, if I came more than three times, I was out for the count. But there was something about a loyal nigga's dick that you didn't get tired of.

"I DON'T SEE why we doing this shit in the first place," Looney mumbled from the passenger seat.

"Yeah, me either, but it seems important to Wiz, so keep your shit together." After days of Wiz bugging me about having this dinner with Nicole, I finally agreed. I pulled up on Looney and forced her to come with me. If I had to sit through this shit, she did, too.

We pulled into Red Lobster and I found a parking spot a few steps from the door. Looney and I walked slowly inside the building and I had to inhale and exhale slowly.

"Welcome. Will it just be you two?" the hostess greeted us.

"I wish," Looney said under her breath and I elbowed her.

"No, we're actually meeting the other two people here. I see them over there, thank you." I cut my eyes at Looney and made my way to the table where Nicole and Wiz were sitting.

"Hey, sissy," Wiz greeted us, causing Nicole to turn around. Nicole's smile dropped slightly when she looked at us.

"I thought you were going to bring the baby." Nicole's voice was full of disappointment, but I didn't care.

"That's why you don't get paid to thought. What's good, sis?" Looney nodded to Wiz and took a seat across from her. I had to shake my head because I knew this damn girl wasn't going to act right.

"No, I wasn't ready for all that and he's with his father anyway. So, what's the reason for you wanting this dinner so bad?" I sat in the empty seat that was across from Nicole. Looking in here face, she looked different from the last time I had seen her. She had a full face, whereas before her cheeks were sunken in and she looked ashy as hell.

"I wanted to get you girls together and apologize. I know it's way past due, but I'm finally getting myself together. I know it'll take a while, but I want to build a relationship with all of you."

"How do we know that this time is going to be different? I can't even count on all our hands how many times one of us wasted money for you to go to rehab only for you to leave. I'm not going through that shit, and I'm sure as hell not putting my child through that."

"I understand and I'm going to prove it to you. I got a job and I'm working to get my own apartment." Nicole smiled and looked like a big kid. A part of me wanted to believe what she was saying, but I was guarded.

"You didn't tell me that," Wiz said, looking at her sideways.

"Because I know you would've tried to step in and do it for me. I want to do it myself."

The rest of the dinner went well besides Looney, who ignored everybody except the waiter. That wasn't my problem, though. I told them I'd get her here, not that I'd make her talk. Nicole and Looney had their own set of issues to work through.

19

ECHO "EJ"

"LIFE DOESN'T GET EASIER OR MORE FORGIVING, WE GET STRONGER AND MORE RESILIENT." -STEVE MARABOLI

"MA! WHERE YOU AT?" I walked into my mama's house with Benson carrying the babies' car seats.

"Echo, you know better than to be making all that noise in my house," my mama fussed. She had a coffee mug in her hand and set it down to hug me.

"Sorry, Ma," I laughed. "You can sit them here and I'll be out in a second," I said to Benson.

"Yes, ma'am. It's nice to see you again," Benson spoke to my mama before leaving.

"You look nice. Where are you headed?"

"I have to meet with my realtor to go look at some buildings. Malik's sister got me motivated to open *The Gallery* back up."

"Why don't you just go back to the old one?" my mama asked me, and I gave her a sideways look.

"There's too much negative energy in there that I can't get out. I want a bigger space anyway for everything I want to do."

"I'm so proud of you, Echo. No matter what happened, I'm glad you didn't just lie down and take it."

"Thanks, Ma. Let me get out of here so I won't be late."

"Okay, baby, we'll talk about the plans for Christmas when you come back." I gave my mama another hug before leaving out.

The first building we were going to see was over in Pilsen. That area always had a lot of traffic, especially around Cermak, so that would be good for business.

"Hey, Echo!" Malani was already waiting when I got there.

"Damn, you early."

"I know, I left out early just in case there was traffic, and I was just too thirsty to wait." We both laughed and walked into the building. The first thing that caught my attention was the large picture windows that were in front. I knew during the day you could get the perfect amount of sunshine inside.

"Hey, Echo girl, I thought I heard someone come in," my realtor, Kelly, spoke as she walked from the back with her clipboard.

"How you doing, Kelly? This is Malani, my business partner." I introduced the two and Malani looked shocked by what I said.

"Nice to meet you," Kelly said, smiling. "So, the owner wants a quarter of a million, but there's a lot of updates that need to be done, especially with this winter. I can probably knock it down about fifty thousand." This is why I only used Kelly for my real estate needs because she made sure I was getting my money's worth.

After touring the building, me and Malani agreed that this would be the perfect spot for the next gallery. After filling out the necessary paperwork, Kelly said she was going to speak with the owners and we'd know something by the end of the week.

"I can't believe you actually want me a part of this. I don't know how I could pay my half, but I will promise you I will. I know if I call my dad—"

"Malani, stop, it's okay. I'm not asking for anything from you, except for your help running this place. Think of it as an early graduation present."

"Aaahh! Oh my God, thank you, thank you, thank you." Malani hugged me tight. My phone rang, and I had to peel Malani's arms from around me to answer it. When I noticed it was my throwaway phone, I just knew something was wrong.

"I got to take this, but I'll be in touch when I hear back from Kelly."

"Okay, see you later." I watched Malani get in her car before I got in mine.

"Speak."

"Your presence is being requested over here," Ron, one of the guys I had watching Elaine, said in an irritated tone.

"Okay, on my way." I hung up and huffed. "I need to go to the party house," I told Benson while I turned my personal phone off. I had nicknames for every place we went, and since Benson had been with me for so long, he always knew what I was talking about.

"I'm not eating that shit until I see Echo! Get your big ass out my face and do what I said!" I heard Elaine's voice yelling the second I walked through the door.

"What the fuck is going on?" I asked, pissed off.

"Boss, she's been screaming like this for hours," Ron explained.

"Echo, sweetie, I've been looking for you. We really need to talk."

"Give us a second." Ron nodded and walked out the warehouse. "What do you want?"

"I thought we were going to sit down and finally have a heart to heart. I know there's some questions you want answered and I'm ready to give you the answers."

"Okay, you can start by telling me who the fuck Rick is and why is he gunning for me?"

"I told you Rick's my husband. I don't know why he's after you, but I'm here to help you with whatever you need. I know you're probably thinking I'm too late and I'm sorry. Just let me explain everything and you can decide what to do with me after that," Elaine begged.

Against my better judgement, I walked over to a table and sat down, signaling for Elaine to do the same. "I'm telling you now if I even feel this is some bullshit, I'm putting you out your misery."

"I promise. What do you want to know first?"

"Do you know where Rick has his trap houses?" Elaine nodded yes. "I want you to write down every last one."

"That's easy. Anything else?"

"Why did you leave me?" I didn't know why that came out, but I really needed to know.

Elaine dropped her head before looking me in my eyes. "I-I was in a bad place back then, Echo. Your dad had just left us, and I was struggling. That was the year I ran into Rick and he swept me off my feet. I wanted so desperately to be loved and taken care of that I would've did anything for him. So when he told me that a child didn't fit in his lifestyle, I had to make a choice. Trust me, Echo, it was the hardest decision I ever had to make, and I regretted it every second." Elaine let two crocodile tears fall from her eyes before wiping them.

"Ron!" I called out.

"Yes, boss?"

"Get her some paper and a pen. I'll be back later for those addresses, and if she starts that screaming shit again, kill her or I'll kill you." I looked Elaine in her eyes before leaving. I was only in there for about twenty minutes and I felt drained. I had Benson take me to get the twins and go back home. Thankfully, my mama had worn both babies out and they slept the entire ride home. Once they were in their cribs, sleeping, I went to take a nap myself.

"Echo. Baby, get up." I felt kisses all over my face and peeked one eye open. Malik was standing over me, looking sexy as hell, only wearing basketball shorts. I noticed how dark it was in the room and saw the sun had gone down.

"Oh my God, how long was I sleeping? Where are the babies?" I threw the covers off me and hopped up.

"Babe, calm down, they're okay. I already checked on them." I let out a deep sigh. "I got us some food, so come eat."

"I must've really been tired. Why didn't you wake me up when you got home?" I asked.

"I tried, but you wouldn't budge, so I let you sleep. Lani told me you all fell in love with a building today."

"Yeah, it's dope and about twice the size of the other gallery. We can do so much more in there, just wait until you see it."

"I love how excited you are about this, baby girl." Malik kissed me on my lips, then pulled my chair out for me.

"I think I'm going to talk to the girls about going legit after this one last hoorah."

"What made you decide that?" Malik set my plate in front of me and my mouth drooled at the steak in front of me.

"I had a sit down with Elaine today, my birth mother, and it opened my eyes to a lot. Besides the fact that she ain't shit." I took a bite of my steak and my eyes rolled to the back of my head. "I can't live having to watch over my back for the next person who decides to come for my head. That's not the life I want to live with my babies."

"Just know whatever you decide, I got your back."

"Thank you, baby daddy. Now enough about me. How was your day?"

"Same ol', same ol'. My sergeant has been asking about meeting you again, and I'm running out of excuses." Malik laughed, but I could tell he was bothered.

"I'm sorry."

"Don't be, I'm good. I like having my personal and professional life separate."

"I love you, Malik."

"I love you, too, Echo." He stopped eating to kiss me on my cheek. We finished eating just as the twins woke up and it was time to be parents.

20

MALIK "DETECTIVE STEVENS"

LAST NIGHT, Echo admitting that she was going to leave the drug game alone made me happy as hell. At this age, I was ready for marriage and working on some more children, and we couldn't do that with Echo still out here, slinging drugs and kicking down doors.

"Leaky? Hey, baby, I wasn't expecting you to come by here." My mama smiled as she opened the door.

"Good morning, Ma. I was coming to see you and Pops before I headed in the office for the day. Is he still here?"

"Yeah, come on, baby. He's sitting down for breakfast. Are you hungry?"

"Nah, I ate already," I said as I followed her to the dining room.

"Look who stopped by, Martin." My dad turned to look at me with raised eyebrows.

"What's going on, son?"

"I just came to talk to the both of you, I won't be long." I took a seat across from him. "Why haven't you made an effort to come see your grandchildren?" I directed that question to my dad.

"I've been busy. How are they?"

"That's bullshit, and you know it is. I can't believe you'd let some stupid feud you got going on in your head stop you from seeing them."

"A'ight, I'm still your father, so watch it."

"Yeah, well, you need to act like it. I don't care if you think Echo is the worse person on this planet, those babies are innocent. MY BABIES are innocent!" I slammed my hand down on the table and stood up to leave. I didn't plan on losing my shit like that, but I couldn't help it.

"Malik, wait." My dad's voice stopped me when I got to the door.

"Yeah?"

"I apologize for making you feel like I don't care about my grandchildren because I do. You're right, they're innocent, and I do want to see them. Extend the invitation to Echo to come by for Christmas Eve dinner." He patted me on the shoulder.

"I'll let her know. Thank you." He pulled me into a hug and I felt a weight lift off my shoulder.

"I messed up and I'm sorry," my dad admitted.

"I'm going to marry her. Can I count on you to be there for me... for us?"

"I'll be there in my best suit."

When I left my parents' house, I felt a million times better. I drove to Mama Lani's house with a smile on my face. Today was the day we were going ring shopping for Echo. I was going to be cliché and propose on Christmas. I wasn't going to lie, I was nervous as fuck when it came to this. I mean, yeah, Echo said she loves me, but did she love me enough to carry my last name?

Ding dong.

I rang the doorbell and stuck my hands in my pocket to keep warm. Today it was only ten degrees outside but felt like it was in the negative with this wind chill. I was glad Echo was staying inside with the twins.

"Come on in out that cold. Where's your scarf? You're going to end up with pneumonia," Mama Lani fussed.

"I left my scarf in the car. I just wanted to make sure you didn't need help with anything." I laughed as I stood at the front door.

"Mmmhhmm. I don't need no help, but you are when you go in the house with pneumonia and Echo put your tail out. I'm ready, honey." She had her lips pursed as she grabbed what she needed and came out. I helped her into the passenger side before walking around to get in the driver's seat. We rode through traffic with the radio playing low. When we got to the jeweler, I looked around at everything. I had never gone ring shopping before and I knew I had to find something that would fit Echo. She was definitely one of a kind and I wanted her ring to be as unique as she is.

"Did you find anything you like?" the saleswoman standing on the other side of the glass counter asked.

"Nah, I think we'll go in another store. You ready?" I looked over at Mama Lani.

"Wait! We do have a new collection that just came in. If you give me a second, I can set them out for you." You could see the desperation in her face. She really wanted that commission. I nodded, telling her I'd wait, and she scurried off to the back.

"We might have to buy a watch or something. I don't think that child is going to let us out of here," Mama Lani whispered. We both laughed as the woman came from the back carrying four black cases.

"These might be more of what you're looking for," she said, opening each case. As I looked over each ring, my eyes landed on a pear shaped ring. "I see you have your eyes on this beauty here. Do you want a closer look?" I nodded.

"Oohh, Malik, this is nice," Mama Lani said as she admired the ring, too.

"I'll take it," I announced as I held it up. "I want a few smaller diamonds added around this one. Her ring size is a seven." After noting everything I wanted done, I handed my credit card over to pay.

"We'll have this ready for you by Christmas Eve. I know your soon-to-be wife is going to love this."

"You can stop laying it on so thick, you made the sale already, sweetie," Mama Lani called her out and I laughed. After leaving the store, we went to the mall to do some more shopping. I made it home around the same time I usually do, and I was happy, so Echo wouldn't ask questions.

"Hey, baby." Echo smiled when I walked into the bedroom. The twins were laid in their bouncer and Echo was sketching in her book.

"This is what you been doing all day?" I asked, pointing to the canvas that was spread across the room.

"Yeah, I just got some motivation and I haven't been able to stop."

"Let me run something by you."

"Oh, God, what is it?" Echo put her pencil down and looked at me suspiciously.

"It's nothing bad, so calm down. I spoke with my dad and he wants us to come over for Christmas to meet the twins."

"And it took him this long to figure that out." Echo rolled her eyes, not even hiding her disdain. "I think we'll pass on that."

"Come on, baby, do it for me. I know shit hasn't been sweet with us, but at least do this for me." I kissed all over her face, and when I got to her neck, Echo let out a small moan. It had been so long since we had been intimate like that, I started getting beside myself and was about to rip the sweats off she was wearing. It was about to get real until Eva started to whine.

"Damn cock blocker already," Echo mumbled when I jumped up to check on Eva, who was looking wide eyed at me.

"Leave my baby girl alone. She just mad because I didn't greet her like I usually do when I get in." I picked Eva up and placed a kiss on her forehead. Elijah was staring up at me, too, so I picked him up as well.

"You just won't be satisfied until they're both spoiled rotten. Keep on and it'll be you staying home to hold them all day." Echo walked out, leaving me in the room.

"Your mama is just jealous. You know I'll hold you all day long," I spoke to the twins.

Christmas Eve

"HELLO?" I answered my phone as I crept out the room. Echo was still sleeping, and I didn't want to wake her up.

"Hello, Mr. Stevens, this is Ruby calling from Forever Treasure. Your ring is ready for pick up."

"Great, I'll be there before closing," I said before hanging up. I checked the time on my phone and saw it was eight in the morning. I was surprised the twins were still sleeping when I checked on them. I learned long ago to never wake a sleeping baby, so I tiptoed out the room.

"Who was that?" Echo asked when I walked back into the room. She was now sitting up in the bed.

"That was Ma making sure we were still coming over."

"Great, I can't wait," Echo said, her tone dripping with sarcasm.

"I promise tonight is going to be okay, and I'll make sure to get you together before we go." I bit my bottom lip as I stood behind Echo, staring at her in the little boy shorts she was wearing.

"How about you give me a sample now to get me through the day?" Echo had her head leaned back on my chest and my hands roamed her body. I stuck my hand in the front of her panties and felt her wetness.

"Take them off," I demanded and stepped back. The second she bent down to remove her panties, I had my face buried behind her. She gripped the side of the sink while I devoured her pussy from the back.

"Aaahh, Leek," Echo moaned as my tongue traveled from her juicy mound to the crack of her ass. I had her cheeks spread wide and enjoyed my meal.

"Mmmm, shit, baby, I'm about to cum."

"Let it go," I said while I was still nose deep in her goodies. When

I tasted the sweet nectar blessing my tongue, I placed a few more kisses below before standing up. I know we had to hurry up before the twins, mainly Eva, woke up screaming. I dropped my shorts and wasted no time diving in. I pumped in and out of her slowly at first before speeding up my strokes.

"Aahh, shit! I missed this shit," Echo screamed. She was throwing her ass back at me and I had to hold on to her waist.

I felt my nut rising and pulled out before I put some more twins inside her. My damn knees got weak and I had to catch myself from falling. We didn't have time to gather ourselves before tiny cries came from the baby monitor.

"I'll go get them started, you take your time getting ready." I kissed Echo on the back of her neck before I washed my hands and pulled my shorts back up. Both babies were screaming by the time I made it to their room. I popped Elijah's pacifier into his mouth while I changed Eva, then I switched.

By the time I had both bottles made, Echo was coming to take over. I told her I had a quick run to make to get some stuff I was supposed to bring to my parents' house tonight. After I got dressed, I hurried up and went to get the ring before going to pick up some bottles of wine. It wasn't like we needed it, but I couldn't come back home empty handed. I hid the ring in my inside pocket before heading home. If everything went as I planned, then next year, Echo would be Mrs. Stevens.

21

NAOMI "NA"

TODAY WAS the day I officially got introduced to Monds' family, and I was a nervous wreck. I didn't know what to wear because I didn't want to be underdressed and have them think I was a bum or overdress and they thought I was a sadity hoe. I finally decided to just keep it simple with some jeans and an off-the-shoulder sweater. DB had just hooked my hair up so that was one less thing for me to stress over.

Jamal had come and picked up JJ yesterday and was bringing him back in the morning. This was our arrangement for the holidays. I hate that it had to come to this, but I wasn't letting no nigga think it was okay to disrespect me. My phone chiming snapped me from my thoughts. I smiled seeing Monds' name pop up.

Cirmondo: I'm on my way to you now.

Me: Okay I'm ready.

I gave myself another once over before sitting down and waiting. Ten minutes later, I heard knocking at the door. I knew it was Monds, but I checked the cameras anyway. You could never be too careful these days.

"What's good, ma? You looking sexy," Monds said, licking his lips. The way he eyed me, it was like he could see through my clothes.

"Thank you, babe, you look good yourself." Monds was wearing a blue button up, khakis and blue loafers. He had a fresh cut, making him look extra daddy-ish.

"Let's get out of here before I end up bending you over and we miss the dinner," Monds whispered in my ear as he gave me a slap on the ass. I grabbed my purse and locked up the house.

We drove for about thirty minutes and my nerves were on a thousand. I stared out the window and didn't even notice my leg was shaking until Monds started rubbing it.

"Calm down, bae, my people are going to love you like I do." The comment shocked me, and I turned to look at him. "Why you looking at me like that?"

"You just said you love me."

"Is that wrong? I mean, we been kicking it for a minute and I know what I feel." He shrugged like it was nothing. I was at a loss for words. "You don't have to say nothing back, ma, I still mean what I said."

Just as I was getting ready to respond, the car came to a stop in front of a brown brick home in Richton Park. The house was well lit with Christmas decorations and I was definitely in the spirit if I wasn't before. Monds parked on the curb, then walked around to open my car door for me. He held my hand tight like he was afraid I would get lost or something.

"Heeyyy, cuz, I was just asking Aunty about you." A tall, model type chick opened the door, smiling from ear to ear.

"What's good, cuz?" We walked into the house and Monds gave her a hug. "This my woman, Naomi. Naomi, this my cousin, Charisma," Monds introduced us and I smiled.

"Hey," I waved, and she brought me into a hug.

"We hug around here. You family if Monds bringing you around."

"A'ight, cuz, let my girl go, she don't run that way," Monds said, laughing and pulling me further into the house. I looked at this Charisma bitch upside her head, ready to lay hands on her. She was over here trying to get free feels and shit.

Monds seemed to have a huge family and they were obviously close. As he introduced me to all his cousins, uncles, and aunties, Monds got nods of approval and I started to loosen up a bit. You know they say if you don't get at least one "I see you" when you meet a guy's family, you popped.

"Hey, Ma." Monds greeted his mother when we finally made it to the kitchen. The way her eyes narrowed, I thought I was going to have to curse her old ass out.

"Well, this must be the young lady that has my son so smitten." She gave me a knowing look.

"Hi are you, I'm Naomi." I moved in front of Monds and took over the introduction.

"Oohh, you're feisty. I like her. You can just call me Celia, sweetie. We'll have to get together and let me pick your brain another time. Go ahead and take your seats at the table." She smiled and shooed us off.

The rest of the dinner went by smoothly and his family was cool as hell. I felt like I was sitting with the hood Cosby's. I was good and drunk by the time I left and was rubbing on Monds' legs the whole drive back to my house.

"I love you, too," I slurred as I stroked his semi-hard penis through his pants. When we made it, we sexed all night until we both passed out from exhaustion. I woke up early the next morning to let Monds out before JJ came back home. It wasn't that I wanted to hide him from Jamal, but I wasn't ready to introduce him to JJ yet.

Knock. Knock.

"I'm coming!" I yelled as I jogged to the door. I saw Jamal standing on the porch, holding JJ's car seat along with some gift bags.

"Merry Christmas," Jamal said, giving me a pathetic smile.

"Merry Christmas," I mumbled. I reached for the car seat, but Jamal walked further in to sit him down.

"JJ wanted to give you some gifts." Jamal handed me the gift bags he had in his hand and I looked at it like it was covered in shit.

"Thanks, you can just put it down."

"Na, can we talk, please?"

"Actually, no, I have to go, and I don't have time for whatever lie you're getting ready to tell me." I didn't have to be at Mama Lani's house until later on, but he didn't need to know that.

"I really want to work on us, Na. We used to be friends before anything." Jamal started spewing his bullshit, making me roll my eyes.

"You should've thought about our friendship before you jeopardized our relationship with that bird. Now I done said all I have to say. You can go." I walked to the door and held it open for him. He walked by with his head held down like I was going to feel bad. Nigga, please.

I locked the door and went to pick JJ up from his seat. Since he was asleep, I took off his snow suit and laid him down while I got ready. Tonight was our family dinner with Mama Lani and the rest of the girls. This was the first one we had with kids, so I knew it was going to be different.

22

ECHO "EJ"

"The worse battle you will ever have to fight is between what you feel and what you know."

"OOOHH, LOOK AT MY LITTLE ANGELS," my mama cooed as she looked at Eva and Elijah in their elf outfits. This year, my mama wanted to be extra and have a theme, so this was what I chose.

"Yeah, your angels are the reason we're so late because they decided to boo boo up their necks as we were getting ready to leave. Thankfully, I bought double."

"That's okay, everybody is waiting in the dining room. You know Nina's tail has been complaining about being hungry," she laughed.

"Finally! Can I make my plate now, Ma?" Looney started up the second we rounded the corner.

"Hey, y'all, merry Christmas." I ignored Looney and went around the table to hug everyone else. Wiz, DB, and Na were the only ones to greet Malik, while Looney and Moe acted like they didn't see him. I was shocked to see Moe's brother Jay here, and even more shocked to see how cozy he and Wiz looked. I was going to get to the bottom of this later.

"Okay, so you know tradition is we always exchange a gift before dinner, and nothing has changed. I think I went overboard for the babies, so I'll just give you the smallest ones to open." My mama came back with an armful of gifts and handed them out. We exchanged our secret Santa gifts before finally sitting down.

After we were done eating, I pulled the girls into a room to talk privately.

"Whatever happened, I didn't do it," Looney blurted out.

"That right there tells me you're guilty of something," I joked. "But no, seriously, I'm stepping down. Anyone who wants to continue in their same position, let me know now."

"I'm happy where I am," Looney spoke up first.

"Me too, I'm good," Moe backed her.

"As far as security and stuff, I'm down to stay, but I want to physically keep my hands clean."

I nodded and looked to DB and Naomi.

"I'm out," Naomi said.

"I just don't want to get my hands dirty either. All other business can stay the same."

"I'm glad we can come to this agreement so easily. Looney and Moe, we can start this transition in the new year. I'll have to set up some private meetings to formally introduce you two to some very important people. Now, I'm just setting the meetings up, it's up to y'all to close." After getting the serious talk out the way, we went back to enjoying everyone else.

Malik had been quiet throughout dinner and I wondered if he was still mad about the dinner we had at his parents' house yesterday. Superintendent Stevens was actually welcoming, it was that sister-in-law of his that made me snap yesterday. She was back to looking at me like I had peed in her cereal, so I had to quickly remind her that I wasn't pregnant and would politely mop the floor with her and her brittle-ass wig. Anyway, back to Malik. He had barely said two words and hadn't even finished eating his food.

"Are you okay?" I whispered in his ear as we all sat around the living room with Christmas carols playing.

"Yeah, I'm good. Let me go to the bathroom right quick," Malik said, tapping my thigh. I was sitting on his lap, so I stood up. I sat back in the seat and watched as the twins were being passed around. Twenty minutes later, Malik came back, sweating like somebody was chasing him. My antennas went up and I was on the defense.

"Okay, what the hell is going on, Malik? Why are you over there sweating so hard?" I stood up and approached him. I guess I was a little loud because all attention was on us now.

"Mama Lani, can you turn the music down for a second?" Malik asked, ignoring my question. If this nigga was on some funny shit, then I was going to have to kill him. He took a deep breath before turning to me and dropping down on one knee.

"Wh-what are you doing? Get up," I whispered and pulled on his arm.

"Echo Janae Brady, I love you more than anything in this world, next to our babies. I had a whole speech I was going to say, but right now, I'm too nervous to even think of what it is," he chuckled nervously and pulled a red velvet box out his pocket. "Echo, will you marry me?"

I stood frozen in place as I looked at the ring he had. It was so perfect, and I knew it would look good on my hand, but I couldn't speak. *Am I even capable of being a wife? Why does this man love me so much and he knows the type of fucked-up person I am?* All these questions ran through my head as all eyes were on me.

"Bae?" Malik looked hurt by my silence. He slowly started to get up, but I stopped him.

"Yes, I'll marry you," I said, releasing the breath I was holding.

"Yessss, bih, let's plan a wedding!" Naomi screamed as Malik slipped the ring on my finger. I didn't even notice they were all crowded around us until now.

Malik picked me up and hugged me tight. He pecked my lips and I held his head, deepening the kiss. The moment was ruined when everyone's phones started beeping at the same time. I pulled my phone out and got heated at the message that flashed across it. The alarm for the warehouse where Elaine was held was going off and I saw it was up in flames.

"What's wrong?" Malik asked, reading my face.

"We gotta go. Ma, can you keep an eye on the babies for a while?" I asked.

"Go handle your business, and please be careful." I hugged and kissed her before rushing out with everybody behind me.

"Ron's not answering the phone, G," Looney fumed.

"Everybody just meet me there and we'll go from there," I directed before hopping in the car with Malik. I gave directions on where to go and I wrapped my hair up on the way.

"Fuuucckkk!!!" I screamed, punching the dashboard over and over again. Malik just looked over at me but didn't speak. We all arrived at the warehouse at the same time and my heart dropped seeing the flames. Firemen were already out, trying to contain the flames that kept growing. I rushed out the car and straight to the police officer I had on my payroll.

"What happened?" Malik asked him, flashing his badge. Officer Dean looked at me, and I nodded for him to speak.

"I don't know, we got dispatched here, saying there was a domestic dispute and got here to see the place up in flames. They pulled some bodies out the fire, but they were already dead."

When he said that, I rushed to see the bodies they had covered in a sheet. The first person I noticed was Ron's half-burned body and my body heated up. It wasn't just that he was killed—the fire hadn't killed him, he had a bullet in the middle of his head. I checked the other three bags and they were the other men I had watching the place.

"Damn," everyone said in unison when they saw what I was looking at.

"This bitch set me up! Wiz, did you get a chance to pull up those addresses I sent to you yesterday?" I fumed and all I saw was black.

"Yeah, sorry, it slipped my mind with this Christmas stuff, I got it on my computer," Wiz rambled as she started pressing buttons on her phone.

"You good, Wiz, relax, we all fucked up. Tomorrow, we're making our move and going to hit every address on that list until we find these mothafuckas. Go enjoy the rest of your night." I turned to walk away and get in the car. Officer Dean already knew what to do with whatever evidence he found that could come back to me.

"Just go home," I said to Malik. I texted my mama and told her I needed her to look after the twins. They had an entire room full of clothes, diapers and formula, so I didn't need to go back there.

"Do you want to talk about what the plan is going to be?" Malik asked, breaking the silence that was in the car.

"I don't have a plan yet, but I know I need to find Elaine and that nigga Rick before I take any more losses."

"You know I got your back, baby girl." Malik reached over and grabbed my hand, kissing the back of it.

"I know, baby, forever." I smiled at him as I thought about our new engagement. Even though the moment was ruined, I was happy.

THE FOLLOWING NIGHT

RATATATATATAT!

Pow! Pow!

"Get the fuck down on the ground! I want to see everybody's hands or you catching a bullet." We were on the third warehouse from the list Elaine had left and I was getting tired of running around the city. The last two we checked had gotten burned to the ground like they had done mine. I was sending a message because I wasn't about to keep playing with these niggas.

"Where that nigga Rick at?" I asked, walking to the nigga who I assumed was in charge of this trap.

"Fuck you, bitch!" he spat.

"Wrong answer," I said, pointing my gun to his head.

Pow!

I sent a shot off and his head exploded all over the wall behind him. "Anybody want to talk to make this easier, or do I have to keep making examples? This extendo is full, so the choice is yours." Nobody said a word, so I went down the line and put bullets in everyone until someone stopped me.

"Okay, wait. Please don't kill me," a nigga begged with his hands in the air.

"You got something useful to tell me?" I looked him square in the eye and he made contact with everyone except me. "I'm not gon' ask again."

"Rick's mansion is in Lincoln Park on Orchard Street. That's all I know," he rushed out.

"Give me his number, and it better be the right one." He nodded quickly and read the number off. I turned and nodded to the crew to finish everybody else off. I sat in the truck as I watched them run out. Seconds later, there was an explosion and I pulled off, satisfied. I dialed the number and it connected through the speakers.

"I was wondering how long it was going to take you to get in touch with me, EJ," who I guess was Rick said.

"Yeah, I was busy. So, now that you have my attention, what do you want?"

"We can do this the easy way and you can just hand over your connects. It's simple." I had to laugh at his stupidity.

"You must not know who I am, Rick. Nothing coming from me will be easy. I'll see you soon." I hung up the phone and smiled. I was going to enjoy torturing this nigga.

I sent out a message for all my soldiers to meet me at the meat market. I didn't want to give them a chance to disappear, so once everyone got there, I instructed them to follow me and we headed to Lincoln Park. Wiz was able to find Rick's exact address and that was where we were going.

"Wiz, turn the alarms off," I whispered into my headset. Wiz was in a van down the street and cut the alarms off on Rick's property. She also had all the cameras on a still frame, so they didn't see me and my crew creeping up.

"It's done," Wiz said after five seconds.

"Go," I instructed to everyone around me before taking off up the stairs. Ten people went around the back of the property and I had five snipers stationed around the property with a perfect view inside. There were another ten men and women behind me as I rushed in the front door.

Boom!

I kicked the door open and started sending shots at anybody in sight. I gave the word to put bullets in anybody in sight. If Elaine was in here, then oh well.

All that could be heard were guns busting all around. I ran upstairs and directly to the big double doors at the end of the hall. I heard a gun cock and Malik snatched me back a second before somebody let a shot off from the room, putting a big ass hole in the door. I looked up at Malik with wide eyes. If he hadn't pulled me back, that could've been my body with the hole in it.

"It's nice to see you again, Echo," Rick yelled out.

"Come out here and let's talk face to face," I taunted.

"Yeah, you can say your last words, bit—"

Pow!

His words were cut off by a gunshot and I looked around at my people, confused. I rushed in the room and saw Elaine standing over Rick, holding a gun. He had a hole in his head the size of a golf ball.

"I wasn't going to let him hurt you, baby," Elaine lied as she let out crocodile tears. If I hadn't watched her make calls on her phone that she thought she was hiding, then I would've fallen for it. She thought she was slick, but I always had eyes on her. If I had watched the cameras earlier, I could've avoided all of this.

Pow! Pow! Pow!

I put one bullet in her head and two in her body and watched Elaine's body fall on top of Rick's. I strolled back out the front door and called the cleanup crew to come get the soldiers I had lost. Once they arrived, I left and went to a warehouse where we burned our clothes and had the trucks stripped.

"Let's go home and celebrate our engagement, baby," I whispered in Malik's ear as he drove. Now that I had gotten the bullshit out of the way, I was ready to finish living my best life with my family. Anything in the past was dead to me, literally and figuratively.

¢

A FEW DAYS LATER

I had spent some well needed alone time with my fiancé, and now it was time to go get my babies. I walked into my mama's house and she still was sitting in the living room, watching the Hallmark channel.

"Ma, didn't you see this already?" I asked, sitting next to her.

"Ssshhh. You watch the same movies over and over, so leave me alone. And if you wake them babies up, I'm going to put you out of here." She cursed me out and hadn't even taken her eyes off the screen. I just shut up and got comfortable next to her.

We watched the full movie before the twins woke up on schedule for feeding. Yes, I was that parent who believed heavily in feeding and sleeping on schedule. This was best to ensure I still got some rest when I needed it.

"How is everything doing, Echo?" my mama asked as she fed Eva.

"With what?"

"Everything. I mean, the way you left out of here on Christmas it seemed serious."

"Yeah, it was, but it's handled."

"Does it have to do with all those fires and bodies dropping that happened the next day?"

"Ma, I don't want you in the middle of nothing I have going on. Just trust that it's handled. Besides, I'm only focusing on my art now."

"That's good because those babies need you with them."

"I know, Ma."

Once I got the babies fed, I got them bundled up and we went home to wait for Malik.

23

MALIK

THINGS WERE JUST GOING BACK to normal, I guess you could say. Echo had gotten up to feed the twins at five this morning, but she never came back to the room. She called Malani around six and they had been talking about how they wanted the new gallery decorated. That went on until about noon when I snatched the phone and made her hang up.

"You not about to do this all morning. Y'all done switched topics like ten times." Echo started laughing at me and I playfully pushed her.

"You so jealous," she said, poking my face.

"I'm not jealous at all, but I want to talk to you." I pulled her into my chest and my hand went right to her plump backside. She could thank me and the twins for that.

"What you do now?"

"Something that I feel is best for everybody," I said honestly.

"Oh, this is serious." The playful look Echo had on her face disappeared as she looked up at me.

"Yeah, it is." I cleared my throat and tried to find my words. "I resigned."

"As in from the force?" Echo asked, stunned.

"It wasn't just your career choice that was a barrier for us, it was mine, too. I figured this way, we can both start over fresh."

"Wow, I'm just shocked and at a loss for words. Are you sure that's what you want to do? What if you get bored?"

"Trust me, I'm good. I had more than enough time to think about what I want to do. Money is not a problem if you're worried about that."

Echo held my face in her hands and looked at me. "I'm not, Malik, I was just worried about you. I don't want you to make that decision thinking that's what I wanted you to do."

"I'm doing this for us. I love you, Echo."

"I love you more."

"How do you feel with your birthday coming up in a few days?" I asked, changing the subject. I had something special planned for Echo already, and I was nervous because I knew how she was with surprises.

"I don't really care to do the big celebration this year. I feel like I'm still recovering from last year."

"Leave it all up to me. I already got some things in motion and you'll love it."

"What is it?"

"It's a surprise, and the first part of the surprise is tomorrow." I could see the wheels turning in Echo's head and had to laugh. This girl didn't know what the meaning of a surprise was.

The next day, I had Benson come get Echo to drive her around for the day. Today started day one of Echo's birthday surprise, and she was getting pampered. She was getting waxed, massaged, and anything else she wanted. After that, she was going shopping and being discreetly fitted for her wedding dress. Thanks to Naomi, who was going to go around with her and make sure everything was done. We were going to be ending our night by having a family dinner at Naomi's restaurant.

Anyway, before all that went on, I had to go meet with my ma and the wedding planner. Thankfully, she had a friend who guaranteed I would have the perfect wedding. I know some women will read this and have their nose turned up. I know my wife-to-be and a dream wedding is never something she dreamed about. If we had just gone down to the courthouse, she wouldn't have complained. But this was our first and damn sure our last marriage, so I wanted it to be special.

I got the twins dressed, which took me damn near an hour to do. Thankfully, I had gotten myself dressed first. I got them bundled up and our first stop was to pick up Mama Lani to look at the banquet hall. This was the first time our mothers would be formally introduced, and I hoped they didn't bump heads about anything.

"Hiiii, you must be Echo's mom. I'm Victoria." My ma greeted us with the biggest smile on her face.

"Nice to finally meet you. You can just call me Lani." They embraced each other before my ma turned to me.

"Take my grandbabies out of that seat, we might be here for a while," my ma instructed. Since I was holding both car seats, I put them down and let the grandmothers take over. "The planner is in the back and we can start the walkthrough now that you two are here. If there is anything that needs to be fixed, we need to know by tonight to make sure everything is ready for the big day." My mama was talking a mile a minute as her heels clacked across the floor. She had been this energetic since I'd asked for her help with everything.

The wedding planner, Melodee, greeted us and started the tour right away. There was a huge open space where the ceremony and the reception were being held and it was big enough to hold at least a hundred people.

"Right now, it looks empty, but the crew will be here tomorrow to bring this place to life. Trust me," the wedding planner assured me as we finished the walkthrough.

"Thank you so much for this. I know everything was last minute," I thanked her.

"You'll be shocked at the amount of weddings I put together in a week or less. I'm the best at what I do, that's why I'm highly recommended." I gave her the other half of the payment I owed before leaving.

"Please don't be late tonight. I know how it can be when there are no kids around." My mama gave me a knowing look and I laughed.

"We won't be late, trust me." I made sure the twins were strapped in their seat before stepping back. Mama Lani and my ma were taking the twins with them to get ready for tonight.

AFTER GETTING FITTED for my tux, I went to get a fresh cut from my barber. Naomi texted me once Echo was on her way home and I got her bath started. I threw in one of her bath bombs and some rose petals.

"Baaaeee. I feel like a brand new person right now." Echo floated through the door with a satisfied grin plastered on her face. I took the bags from her hand and gave her a kiss.

"I'm glad you enjoyed your day, but your surprise isn't over yet. I have a nice, warm bubble bath waiting for you to get in."

"Where's the twins? It's quiet, and I know it's time for them to eat."

"Don't worry about that right now, they're with Mama Lani."

"Ohhh, you really going all out for li'l ol' me, huh?"

"I'll do anything for you, baby, never forget that," I said seriously as I led her to the bathroom. I helped her strip out her clothes and I made sure to run my hands slowly over every inch. Echo's skin was smooth, from her face down to her feet. I had never been a man who was into all that foot-in-the-mouth stuff, but I'd suck Echo's toes until they pruned. That was how much I loved every part of her.

"Malik, don't start spoiling me like this. I might want this done every day," Echo moaned as I fed her a strawberry.

"I don't know about every day, but you might get it a few times out the month." Echo shot me an evil glare before closing her eyes back.

Once the water started to get cold, I turned on the shower and hopped in with her. We were on a time schedule, but the way my dick was sticking up, I needed to relieve some pressure. The second I closed the shower door, I pinned Echo against the shower wall and started kissing her neck.

"Ohhh, shit," Echo moaned with her hand on the back of my head. I had a hand on her freshly shaven kitty and started playing with her clit. I wanted to take my time in here because there was no telling when we'd have some more alone time like this, but knowing that my mama would pop up over here if I was late had me rushing.

"Gggrrr," I growled against Echo's neck as I lowered her onto my hardness. I guided her up and down slowly at first, then I pounded into her. The sounds of our skin slapping and moans were all that could be heard in the shower. I felt my nut rising and it took everything in me to pull out. I knew I wasn't ready for more kids yet, so I pulled out and let my nut shoot out on the shower floor.

"Fuck, if we wasn't on a time schedule right now, I would have you stretched all over this house. Come on and shower."

Smack!

I popped Echo on the ass, then set her on her feet. We washed up and stepped out the shower.

"I'm ready to just sleep now. My body has never felt this relaxed," Echo whined as she laid across the bed in her bra and panties.

"We got dinner reservations, so come on, baby." I handed her the dress she had picked up today and slowly rolled out the bed.

It took us another forty minutes to get dressed, and for Echo to put her makeup on. The dress Echo was wearing was red and hugged her in all the right places. I was almost ready to cancel the dinner and finish our night, rolling around in the sheets. Instead of giving in to temptation, I waited at the door for Echo.

Benson was waiting outside for us to take us to Rich Dreams. I could see the excitement on Echo's face and I just hoped that stayed with her when I told her that we were getting married in two days.

24

ECHO "EJ"

"So, I close my eyes to old ends. And open my heart to new beginnings."

"MALIK, I swear you better not let me fall." This crazy nigga had blindfolded me in the car and now had me walking, following the sound of his voice.

"You not about to fall, just come on." I could hear the laughter in Malik's voice, further irritating me.

"Surprise!" I jumped and looked around the room. Naomi, DB, Looney, Wiz, and Moe were sitting at the table with my mama, Liz, the twins, Malani and Malik's parents. I was happy his brother hadn't come with that wife because I wasn't going to try to save her from the ass whooping she had earned the last time I'd seen her.

"Happy almost birthday, boo," Wiz squealed as she hugged me.

"Thank you, you looking sexy," I said, eyeing the tight jumpsuit Wiz had on.

"You know I had to look the part today. I don't think y'all

would've appreciated me in my usual sweatpants and t-shirt." We both laughed, and I hugged her again before speaking to everyone else.

Malik and I were sitting at the head of the table and I felt like royalty. This was probably the most lowkey birthday dinner I'd ever had in my adult life. I think I loved Malik even more for putting this together.

"This is a nice place here," Superintendent Stevens spoke as he looked around the restaurant.

"Yeah, thanks," Na answered dryly. She was sitting there with Monds, looking the happiest I'd seen her in a while. I guess it was true; you get a certain glow when you let go of a fuck nigga.

As dinner went on, everyone seemed to be in their own conversation until Malik stood up, clinking his glass.

"Ahem. I want to start by thanking every one of you for clearing your schedule to be here tonight, it means a lot. Echo, I know you think this is just a birthday dinner, but it's much more than that." Malik turned towards me completely and smiled. "You know I couldn't wait until you carried my last name, so I have it set to happen on your birthday. I want you to go into the new year as my wife. What do you say?"

"Are you serious?" I looked at Malik, then at everyone sitting at the tables. The smiles I got back let me know that he was serious. I felt myself getting emotional and had to wave my tears away. "Yes, babe, I'm with it," I finally answered his question. Malik pulled me up from my seat to kiss me.

"All right, y'all can save all of that for the wedding night," Looney interrupted the moment, causing everybody to cut their eyes at her. Her ass couldn't be serious for anything.

¢

Wedding day

Knock. Knock.

"Come in," I called out as I wrapped myself in my robe.

"Good morning to the beautiful bride. I am here to get your hair and makeup together, so have a seat, my love." DB smiled as she dragged her case of hair and makeup products into my room.

Last night, me and the girls stayed at The W and had my bachelorette party. All we did was get drunk and high and turn up on our own. Since it was New Year's Eve, when it was time for the countdown, I made Malik come to the hotel for my New Year's kiss. Naomi had a fit, but she finally agreed after making sure we were both blindfolded. I didn't care because I had gotten my kiss and now I was getting ready to marry the love of my life.

"I think I'm going to pin the front and give you some wand curls in the back. I know you haven't seen your dress yet, but it'll go perfectly."

"How is it that y'all were able to keep this from me?" I asked, astounded. These bitches couldn't hold water, but all of a sudden, nobody could talk.

"Hey, it was all your hubby. I just got a text the morning of the dinner saying my presence was needed and not to be late. Come on and sit down so I can get to work." DB started laughing and pointed to the vanity in the room.

I had fresh bundles in, so it didn't take DB any time to curl my hair and pin the top back with a diamond hair pin. She told me that was my something new. She was such a white girl and I had to laugh at her. There was another knock at the door and Naomi came in with Curtis trailing behind her.

"Damn, you was in on it too?" I asked him.

"Uh, yeah, hoe. Who did you think was going to slay you for yo' big day? I think I'm offended." Curtis put his hand on his chest like he was offended.

"Don't even start with your mess. Let me see my dress," I urged.

"Oop, don't be rushing me. You better be lucky I love you." Curtis was being dramatic as always, rolling his eyes and popping his lips.

Curtis took a garment bag off the rack he had rolled in and unzipped it, revealing the prettiest ivory-colored dress I'd ever seen. I had never really thought about my dream wedding dress, but this would definitely be it. I stepped in the dress and it fit me perfectly, which I wasn't surprised by. The strapless sweetheart neckline showed off my long neck Curtis always fawned over. The back had a corset look, and had a long train, giving me a princess feel. I was just glad it wasn't white.

Once I had the dress on and Curtis made some adjustments with me in it, I was covered in a cape for DB to do my makeup.

Standing in the mirror, staring at myself, I was on the verge of tears.

"You better not start crying after I just packed this makeup up," DB warned from behind me.

"I'm so ready for this," I admitted with a smile. "I had some doubts about being a wife, but I know I love Malik and would spend forever with him."

"Ohhh, look at Echo getting all sentimental and stuff." DB dabbed away some fake tears and I stuck my middle finger up at her.

"Let's go before your mother-in-law calls me again," Naomi said, walking into my room. When she looked up at me, her eyes started watering. "Echoooo."

"No, Naomi, get out and get in the limo. Here we come." DB pushed her out the door before she got started. "Somebody is coming to pack your room up, so just grab your purse and junk."

I slipped my feet in some Crocs and grabbed my clutch. I know it was my wedding, but I stuck my .380 in there anyway. I followed DB outside and to a stretch Rolls-Royce Phantom. Benson was holding the door open for us and his smile was stretched across his face when he saw me.

"You look beautiful, Ms. Brady. I guess I should get used to calling you Mrs. Stevens now," Benson beamed.

"Thank you, Benson, you look handsome yourself." I got in the back with the girls and they were all in their own conversation.

"EJ, you looking like a whole snack," Moe sang when she noticed me sitting there. That caused everyone else to turn around and look at me.

"I told y'all I was about to lose it upstairs. I'm so happy for you, bestie," Naomi smiled. She was blinking fast, I guess trying not to let any tears fall.

Twenty minutes later, we pulled up to a venue and I was being ushered out the backseat.

"Hey, Echo, I should've known this was for you. That name isn't very common." Melodee, my homie Dame's wife, spoke as she led me to a room.

"How did they get you in on this?" I asked her as I slipped on my pointed toe heels.

"I know your mama-in-law. She always has me planning some pointless party for somebody. You know I'm not turning no bag down from them," Melodee laughed.

"I can see why Dame married you. Y'all like the same person."

"Thank you, now come because your husband is waiting for you." Melodee looked over my appearance and placed my veil on my face. My heart was beating erratically as I got to the room where Malik was waiting.

I watched the girls walk into the room in a single line and I waited behind the closed door. I heard someone start playing the piano and the doors opened for me. Melodee waved me off and mouthed, "walk," to me.

As I walked down the aisle, my eyes connected with Malik's. I don't know if he could see my eyes through this veil, but I saw his clearly. He looked sexy in his fitted suit. I knew he had gotten his hair cut the other day, but he still had that fresh cut look. When I was in arm's reach, Malik reached out to me and I took his hands. He pulled the veil back and stared at me, and I saw the tears he was holding.

"Today is a celebration. A celebration of love, of commitment, of friendship, of family, and of two people who are in it forever." The officiant started with his opening statement and I was still stuck, staring into Malik's eyes. That moment when you find that person who loves you, even knowing your every flaw, never let them go.

"Will you, Malik, take this woman to be your wedded wife?" Hearing the officiant ask Malik that question snapped me from my thoughts.

"I will."

"Will you, Echo, take this man to be your wedded husband?"

"I will."

"May I have the rings, please?" Naomi handed him the rings and took her spot behind me. "Malik, please repeat after me: I give you this ring as a daily reminder of my love for you."

"I give you this ring as a daily reminder of my love for you," Malik repeated and put the band on my finger.

"Now, Echo, please repeat after me: I give you this ring as a daily reminder of my love for you."

"I give you this ring as a daily reminder of my love for you." I put Malik's band on his finger and we smiled at each other.

"Look at each other and remember this moment in time. By the power of your love and commitment, and the power vested in me, I now pronounce you, husband and wife. You may kiss each other now."

Our family and friends cheered as we shared our first kiss as husband and wife. I was still trying to recover from the kiss when Melodee dragged us to the room to get our pictures taken.

When we stepped back into the room the guests were in, there were more people inside than it originally was. The DJ introduced us as Mr. and Mrs. Stevens and we went to the middle of the room for our first dance.

I can't believe it's true,
I'm standing here in front of you, and you are here with me.
So unbelievable.
I'll never let you go, my heart is yours for keeps.
Let's make a vow (Let's make a vow baby)
Right here and now (Here and now)

I laid my head on Malik's chest as he led our first dance to K-Ci & JoJo's song "This Very Moment". I never felt safer than I did right now, wrapped in Malik's arms. It seemed as if our hearts were beating in sync now. I couldn't believe I was someone's wife now.

25

NAOMI "NA"

"YOU BETTER NOT START CRYING AGAIN," Monds whispered in my ear as we watched the couple's first dance.

"Shut up, this is a beautiful wedding." I rolled my eyes and discreetly wiped my tears away.

After their first dance, the DJ opened the floor to everyone else. I was surprised when Monds stood up and asked me to dance. I mean, I knew he was different from what I was used to, but the stuff he did still shocked me at times. The DJ started playing "Best Part" and H.E.R.'s voice flowed through the room. Monds' cologne had me mesmerized as we moved slowly around the dance floor. I loved when he wore Y by YSL cologne, and I think that was why he had gone and racked up on it.

"Have you ever thought about what you would want your wedding to be like?" Monds asked. The question threw me off and I stopped moving. Monds had a hand on my lower back, so he kept guiding me. "Just answer the question."

"Yeah, but that was when I was with my baby's father. I think I would want something much different now," I admitted.

"I always saw myself as a family man. I always saw how a woman is supposed to be treated because my father loved my mother up until he took his last breath. I want that with you."

It was hard fighting my tears now. "I want that, too, I just can't take any more heartache." Monds dabbed away at my tears and kissed me slowly.

"I can guarantee I will never do anything to hurt you, and you know I'm a man of my word, Naomi." All I could do was stand there and smile.

I looked over at where Echo and Malik were and noticed an older looking man dressed in a pressed uniform approaching them. From the look on Malik's face, he wasn't expecting him, and Echo didn't look happy at all.

"I'll be back," I said to Monds. The other girls must've noticed the same thing because they walked towards Echo until I waved them off. I interrupted whatever conversation they were having when I cleared my throat.

"Sorry to disturb you, but the rest of your guests would like to see you." I smiled at Echo, forcing her to smile back.

"Right, it was nice meeting you," Echo said to the guy as she walked away with Malik behind her. Malik didn't even bother speaking.

"I don't know who you are or who invited you, but you need to leave." I nodded to security and they stood behind him.

"I'll be seeing them again, it's okay. It's Sergeant Gill, by the way." He held his hand out for me and I just looked down at it. He caught the hint and left.

"What was that all about?" Looney asked.

"I don't know, but now is not the time to find out. Echo is going to enjoy the rest of her day, and tomorrow, you two can make sure there's no problems coming your way. Enjoy today, have a drink. Tomorrow is a new day." I walked away and joined Monds back at our seats.

"You good?" Monds gave me a questionable look when I sat down.

"Yeah, everything's good." The servers started to bring food out, so everyone started taking their seats. "I'm just glad I'll be done with that side of things and can focus on my business and my baby."

Echo didn't want to leave the twins again to go on a honeymoon, so Malik had a staycation set up for them downtown. We were all going to step in and help Mama Lani until they got back.

MONDAY STARTED a new week and it was the first week I was opening Rich Dreams for brunch. I hadn't really had the chance to put on my chef hat in a while, so I was loving being in the kitchen right now.

"Boss lady, you're needed out at table twelve," my hostess announced, then rushed back out the kitchen.

"Lola, take over for me." I took my apron off and washed my hands quickly. There were some renovations done and each table had a little more privacy. I wanted to attract the business class as well as my neighborhood dope boys.

When I saw who was waiting for me at table twelve, I smiled. "Hey there, handsome. What do I owe this visit?" Monds stood up and wrapped me in his arms.

"I knew you was gon' be too busy for me, so I decided to come to you." Monds gave me a few pecks before pulling back. "I'm not going to hold you. I brought some associates here to discuss business. I'll see you later on, right?"

"My plans haven't changed, just call me when you're on your way." I walked back to the kitchen smiling like I had just won the lottery. It was crazy how that one quick visit from Monds could make my day go that much better.

Once the restaurant closed up after brunch, we cooked a staff meal and relaxed until it was lunch time. I went to my office to call and check on JJ, who was with Mama Lani. I was hesitant to leave him because I didn't want to overwhelm her since she had Eva and

Eli, too. Before I could dial Mama Lani's number, I got a call from an unknown number. I wasn't going to answer, but I couldn't miss a business opportunity.

"Hello, this is Naomi."

"Hey, Na, it's me." I stared at the phone to look at the number again.

"Who is this?"

"It's your mama, girl, stop playing. I tried to reach out for Christmas, but I couldn't get through," Nicole said.

"Aw, yeah? Well, what's up?"

"I have these Christmas gifts for the baby I wanted to make sure he got. Can I stop by sometime?"

"Nicole, I'm in the middle of something right now, I'll call you back." I said the first excuse I could think of.

"Oh, okay then. I understand if you don't want to forgive me yet, I'll just give the stuff to Nadia." I hated hearing how pathetic she sounded on the phone, but she had dug her own hole.

26

MALIK

"BAE GET your phone before I break it." Echo woke me up when she slapped me with a pillow.

"Just silence it," I mumbled and rolled over.

"I tried that, and he just keeps calling. Now get up before I have to break your phone." My phone stopped ringing, so I closed my eyes. When it rang again, not even a minute later, I got up to answer it.

"Hello?"

"Stevens, we need to meet and have a conversation," Sergeant Gill said into the phone.

"About what? Just tell me now over the phone." I sat up in the bed and wiped the sleep from my eyes.

"It's best if we talk in person. I'll send the address." He hung up before I could respond, leaving me confused.

"Babe! I need to go meet with my sergeant and see what he wants." Echo was in the closet and she came out to look at me.

"He's not your sergeant anymore. Why do you have to meet him somewhere?"

"I don't know, but it seem like it's serious." My phone lit up and I saw Sergeant Gill had sent me an address.

"There's something about him I don't trust, but if you feel you have to do this, then okay. You just better be back in time to meet with the realtor." Echo said what she had to say and went back into her closet.

"I'll be back in time." I headed to the bathroom to empty my bladder and handle my hygiene. Echo had some clothes laid out for me, so I put them on. I kissed her and the babies before going to meet Sergeant Gill.

I made it to a small diner he had sent me the address to and found him sitting in a booth. "How it's going, sir?" I slid in the booth and made sure my clothes were straight.

"I'm glad you were able to meet me. You know I was a little confused when I got your registration on my desk, but now it's clear why you did. How long have you been working for EJ?"

"I don't know what you're talking about. I don't work for anyone right now." I sat across from him, unbothered.

"Echo Brady. When you got that case, I just knew you were going to be the one to break the case and do what many have failed to do. Is your father apart of all of this as well?"

"Again, I don't know what you're talking about. Do you care to elaborate?"

"The Coke Gurls. The Feds have been building a case for the longest and you almost messed it up. They came to me because they suspected there was a leak in the department, but I never would've expected it to be you."

"You were there through the entire investigation like I was. Echo was cleared of all charges with prejudice. I know there's probably a lot of heat on you with elections that just passed, but you're barking up the wrong tree."

"You really love her, huh?" Sergeant Gill had a smug look on his face that I wanted to smack off.

"Tread lightly," I warned.

"Well, I tried to help you. Don't say I didn't." Sergeant Gill stood up and patted my shoulder.

"Hold on. What do you want?" I knew there had to be something in it for him to want to warn me.

"As you know, the pay is terrible. All I need is a small monthly payment of twenty thousand and this problem disappears," he said like I just had that money sitting around the house.

"I can see you're thinking about it, so I'll give you time, but not too much. Congratulations again, the wedding was beautiful." I was left stuck until I got a text from Echo, telling me to hurry up. This nigga hadn't even left money for the food he was eating, so I left a twenty before going to pick Echo up.

"I was about to have Benson come get us. You know I hate being late." Echo was pushing the car seats to my chest the second I unlocked the door. She shooed me back out and I waited for her to lock up.

"We still got about forty five minutes before we supposed to be there, just chill, mama."

"No, I can't wait to see these houses. I feel like the walls are closing in on me. I don't even have all of my things there—"

"A'ight, man, damn, I get it." I interrupted Echo before she could keep talking shit about my house.

"Don't be mad at me," Echo laughed. "You know I love your house, baby, but we just need to find a home that works best for our family."

"Yeah, okay." I scoffed at Echo's attempt to clean up her insult.

It took us thirty minutes to get to the Lincoln Park neighborhood where the first few places are. The first place we met the realtor at was a condo. I could tell by Echo's face that she didn't like it when we pulled up, but she walked through anyway.

"I'm not sure what vision you thought I was looking for, but this isn't really it. I want a home, with some land around it, not this." Echo waved her arms around the furnished condo.

"That's cool, Echo, you know I have a few more listings for you today. I'll send you the addresses." The realtor tapped away on her phone and packed up the papers she had brought with her.

The next stop was a house that reminded me a lot of my parents' house. Echo didn't like it because of how close the other homes were, so we didn't even look inside. An hour later, we were finally getting out the car to see the inside of a place.

"This might be it, bae, I can feel it. What do you think?" Echo smiled as we walked around the house. Let me stop saying 'house' because it was a damn mansion. There were eight bedrooms and nine bathrooms with a huge backyard that reminded me of something we saw on HGTV somewhere.

"I'm feeling this, but what's the price looking like?"

"Come on, babe, I wouldn't have us looking at something that wasn't in our price range." Echo turned and batted her eyes at me. I smelled the bullshit she was spitting at me.

"Soooo, did I do good?" The realtor, whose name Echo reminded me was Kelly, came in the kitchen where we were.

"You definitely did good. You should've started with this one," Echo joked. "You have all of our information, right?"

"Yes, I do."

"Bae, do you want to make an offer?" Echo looked up at me with wide eyes like I was going to tell her no. I knew better.

"Yeah, we do. Does that mean we don't have to go look at nothing else?" I looked from Echo to Kelly and back to Echo.

"No, we can go get something to eat now. Thank you so much, Kelly, you already know what to do."

"Yes, ma'am, you should be hearing from me soon." Kelly waited for us to leave before she got in her car and started making calls.

"So, what's the normal routine with you two? We didn't speak numbers or nothing." I was driving us to grab something to eat before going home.

"Whatever the asking price is, I offered fifty thousand or more lower and throw cash on the table. Kelly always knows how much to ask for, depending on how thirsty the owners are. She'll get whatever the difference is, so trust me, she's motivated."

I had nothing to say to that, so I just shook my head, letting her know I understood. There was so much to my wife I had to learn.

"So, what did the sergeant say?"

"Aw, shit." I had gotten so wrapped up with Echo and house hunting I had forgotten all about seeing Sergeant Gill. "Well, he wants to get paid twenty thousand a month to help get the Feds off your back."

Echo burst out laughing, holding her stomach and everything. "That's the problem with these fake law abiding citizens: greed. What makes that nigga think he deserves anything but a bullet for playing with me?" Echo's face turned serious.

"He's saying he has the power to decide whether you're in jail for life or not."

"Okay, tell him I'll pay."

"You don't have to do that—"

"No, it's fine. I'll let his greed be his demise."

I let the conversation die as I pulled up to Portillo's driveway. It seemed like no matter what, Echo would always get pulled back into that life we were trying to escape.

ECHO "EJ"

"I want to raise a glass to EJ. If it wasn't for every risk you took back in the day, we wouldn't be where we are today." Looney raised her glass and everybody else did the same.

"Not to mention, you paved the way for us and got these niggas to realize we can do what they can, only better." Moe added her two cents in, then brought her glass to her mouth. I took a sip from my Hennessy and put it back down on my table.

After months of showing Looney and Moe the ropes, I was officially done in the drug game. All of my ex-business partners were in attendance, and I was surrounded by love. Tomorrow, me and Malik were finally going on that honeymoon we never got to go on. For a week, it was just going to be me and my husband, exploring each other on a private island.

We officially opened the doors to Brush'd Chi and opening night, we raised more than thirty thousand dollars that was given to the

Chicago Public School. I was keeping the same tradition to have the show once a month to donate to any charity or family we chose.

The violence in the city had died down a lot, so I felt comfortable with Looney and Moe handling business how it was supposed to be.

"All right, come on, Malik. I'm ready to go see my babies one more time." My mama was at our house, watching the twins, and I just wanted to kiss their little faces.

"Damn, stop walking so fast." Malik was about four steps behind me, but I wasn't slowing down. If he knew what I had planned, he'd hurry up, too.

The second I stepped out the building, I had guns pointed in my face. By instinct, I pulled my gun out and I learned that was the worst thing I could've done. I heard someone yell, "Gun!" before shots rang out. I ducked down and peeked up to see Sergeant Gill leading the damn pack. This nigga had been playing us for months and taking my money. That sent me over the edge and I stood with my gun pointed. I wasn't going down without a fight. I started firing my gun at Sergeant Gill until I felt that first shot.

The first one hit my right shoulder, making my arm fall to my side. I grabbed the gun with my other hand and let shots off before I was hit by more bullets. I hit the ground and stared up into the night sky. What's the fucking irony that the Feds would move in on me the day of my retirement party?

"Echo! Baby, oh my God, I'm so sorry I froze." Malik was kneeled on the ground next to me, crying. I saw him shed some tears when the twins were born, but now, he was bawling. I felt tears roll down my face and I tried to talk.

"Bae," was all I was able to get out before I started coughing.

"Sshhh, don't try to talk. I hear the ambulance coming. Just hold on. Please don't leave me," Malik begged.

I heard the ambulance sirens grow closer as I went in and out of consciousness. My eyes closed and when I opened them up, Naomi was staring down at me, crying. She had makeup running down her face and I felt my heart breaking. My eyes closed again, but when they opened this time, I was in the back of the ambulance. I saw the medic's lips moving, but all the words sounded jumbled.

"Everything is going to be okay, ma'am," I heard the medics say into my ear before my eyes closed again. It felt like I just blinked, and I was in the hospital. There were so many doctors and nurses running around me, I was getting dizzy. My body started shaking like crazy and the monitors around me started beeping.

"She's coding!"

NAOMI "NA"

I felt like I was in a nightmare that I couldn't wake up from. I couldn't get that image of Echo out my head with all those holes in her. Those pigs shot her like she was an animal in the street. If she died, I was going to make sure to visit each one of them bitches and make their family pay.

"Na, what happened? What happened?" Looney walked up to me and her eyes were red like she had just got done smoking.

"They shot her, man. They fucking shot Echo. There was so much blood. I don't think she's going to make it!" I screamed as I broke down crying again. I slid down to the floor and hugged my legs. Looney reached out to touch me and her hands were shaking.

"Don't fucking say that, Naomi! She is going to make it. Don't fucking say that again," Looney snapped and wrapped her arms around me. I knew she was crying because I felt the wetness on my shirt.

I didn't know how long we were crying, but I fell asleep and was woken up by Looney shaking me. I got up, ready to snap until I saw her pointing to two doctors who were standing in the private waiting room we were in.

"I'm sorry, we did everything we could, but she lost too much blood, too fast. She was hit in some—"

"Fuck! Fuck! Fuck! Fuck!" Malik screamed as he punched the wall over and over again. The entire room was crying as we stared at the doctors. I was waiting for them to say they had the wrong room. There was no way my best friend was gone.

"Can we see the body?" I asked before the doctors crept out the room.

"Give us a second to get her cleaned up and you can come back," the taller one said, and I nodded. Twenty minutes later, those same doctors came and showed us to the room Echo was in. She was still hooked up to the machines, but they were muted. I could clearly see the flatline on the screen, though.

We all stood around her bed in silence, just staring at her. All that could be heard were sniffles from everybody. Looney was crying so hard, she passed out and Wiz had to get the nurses for her. The sun came up and we were now sitting around Echo's bed. The doors opened and Mama Lani walked in. Her face was flushed, and she had fresh tears coming down.

"Ooohh, my sweet Echo," Mama Lani sobbed. Malik gave her his seat and he stood. "They called me because you all won't leave. I can't believe my baby is gone, but she nor you all can sit here. Malik, you have two babies who need you to be strong right now. Naomi, you have a handsome son and two little sisters who need you. We have to let them take her."

Hearing those words had everyone in tears again. There was no way this was real. Mama Lani dragged each one of us out the room by our arms after a while. There was a driver waiting to take us to our own homes. When I got to my house, I saw Monds' car parked in the driveway. He hopped out and opened my door for me. I fell into his arm and he picked me up, carrying me bridal style into the house.

Monds carried me to my master bath and sat me on the toilet. I watched him as he turned on the bath and threw a bath bomb in the water. Next, he helped me undress before he undressed as well. He carried me to the tub and stepped in, still holding me in his arms. I cried as Monds held me and rubbed my back. I wanted all of this to be some kind of sick joke. I didn't think I could live without my best friend on the Earth.

We stayed in the water until it turned cold, then Monds led us to the shower. He washed us up, then we got out. I had on a robe and Monds had a towel wrapped around his waist and we laid in the bed just like that.

The last few days had been a blur. I hadn't been able to sleep since I'd been home, and now, I was forced to bury my best friend. Mama Lani had called and threatened me, saying I better be up with my ass washed and my hair done by the time my driver came. I knew better than to go against what she said, so I got up and got dressed. We were all wearing purple and gold to honor Echo. Curtis had made us all dresses and he joked saying Echo was going to kill him for making us something.

"The car just pulled up, baby." Monds walked up to me and wrapped his arms around my waist. He never left my side and I loved him even more for that.

"Okay, I'm ready." I grabbed my gold clutch and we left out.

All of the girls pulled up at the same time and we walked in together. As we walked to the front, I noticed Jamal sitting in the second row and I smiled at my little fat baby in his suit. I sat next to Mama Lani and she grabbed my hand. She decided to have a closed casket because she knew we couldn't take seeing her like that again.

The service seemed to go by in slow motion and it was torture. Every sad song the choir sang broke my heart even more. I didn't even know if I had any more tears left. When we got to the cemetery, I lost it completely. This was what made it all real. I was burying her, and I would never be able to see her again.

Nicole was at the burial and she looked like she was crying, too. I approached her, and she pulled me into a tight embrace. Shockingly, I accepted it and hugged her back. Losing Echo opened my eyes to a lot, and I didn't want to live on holding any grudges.

Looney, Wiz, DB, Moe, and I all put something special on Echo's casket to bury with her. I said a prayer and placed a kiss on top of the gold casket. I walked to Malik's mother, who was watching the twins, and I grabbed them from her. This was one time Eva wasn't screaming at the top of her lungs. I hugged them tight before getting back in the car to go home. I couldn't watch them put her in the ground. I texted Jamal and told him to bring JJ home to me. I just wanted to stay home and cuddle with my man and my baby.

EPILOGUE

One year later

ECHO "EJ"

"If you don't sacrifice for what you want, what you want becomes the sacrifice."

Sitting on the beach as the waves hit the rocks, I was zoned out. After everything that went down with the police, I knew I wasn't getting away from that with a slap on the wrist, so I did what I had to do for my babies and my husband. I hated being away from my babies, but it was for the best. When I was "dead", I was actually in a medically induced coma to heal from my injuries. Once I had half of my strength back, I reached out to get Malik and the twins here, and Colombia had been our home ever since.

Looney and Moe were still running the Chi tighter than ever. Although I was retired, I still got my cut every month, I just didn't get my hands dirty. I was making millions by just laying in the sun all day.

Wiz had to get everyone new identities just in case the Feds or anybody else tried to come after them, and so far, it had been quiet. Come to find out, Sergeant Gill had died that night and I was glad.

Apparently, he was setting us up with this whole you need to pay me routine he pulled. He was really their witness. With him dead, and me dead, so was their case.

Brush'd Chi was being run by Malani and it was more successful than it ever had been. I guess my death had a lot to do with that.

My mama visits every other month and makes me FaceTime her every day, so the twins won't forget her. Those were her words. I was thinking about just having her move down here. Our compound had more than enough space for my mama to have her privacy.

You would be shocked to know that Superintendent Stevens, my father-in-law, was the one to orchestrate my move out here to Colombia. He was the first face I saw when I opened my eyes. He told me that he didn't save me, he saved Malik. He knew if I were to go to jail for the rest of my life, it would've killed Malik on the inside. When my husband saw me, he held on to me for the entire day, literally. The only time I got privacy was on the toilet. He kept telling me how he was never letting me go again and I believed him. I felt the same way, though.

It was an adjustment being here, but having my family made it all worth it. I might be a devoted mother and wife now, but I was a Coke Gurl forever.

The End!

AFTERWORD

A Note From The Author

Book number fourteen is complete! These ladies came to show that men aren't the only ones who can run a successful drug empire and still find love. Although their journey wasn't an easy one, they showed strength and handled their business. I hope you all enjoyed reading this book as much as I enjoyed writing it. Don't forget to leave reviews!

Love,

AJ

Let's Chat!
Facebook: AJ Dix
Instagram: ashley_jovan
Twitter: Bunniepjs
Like my author page on Facebook @AuthoressAJDix and join 'JAY's Readers Group' for sneak peeks, discussions and giveaways!

ALSO BY AJ DIX

More great reads from AJ:

Shorty Fell in Love with a Dope Boy 1-3
In Love with the King of Chicago 1-2
He Wants a Li'l Baby That's Gone Listen 1-2
Incapable: If I Fall in Love Again
I'll Go Round For Round Over My Thug
Married To A B-More Bully 1-3

COMING 09/10!